Jacky U

Enjoy

Winds from the Mountains

by

Fred Wascura

Fred Wascura

2

Copyright 2015 Fred Wascura

All rights reserved

ISBN-13:978-1514104927

ISBN-10:151410492X

All rights reserved. This book is a work of fiction. Names,
characters, businesses, organizations, events, and incidents are
either the product of the author's imagination or are used fictitiously.
Resemblance to actual persons is coincidental.

Dedicated to our ancestors who came from afar with brave optimism to build a better life for the next generations.

Author's Note

This fictional story is based on historical events and inspired by stories heard about the past from relatives. It is the story of the immigration and coming to American of the poor people of the Carpathian Mountains and those that stayed behind. These related families on both sides of the Atlantic found themselves caught up in world events and changing borders. These families of the mountains were Rusyn.

Chapter One

Dreaming

There exists a beautiful world near the Tatra Forest in the Carpathian Mountains under snow white peaks, a town named Osturna. People live here in poor wood houses, traditional in religion and pure Rusyn in old heritage. Although they are not so rich and the people are not well educated, the atmosphere is friendly and welcoming in this spring of 1896. Osturna is located in the Spis district in the Slovak area of the Austro-Hungarian Empire. The village stretches for over five miles along the northernmost road near the Polish border. The High Tatra Mountains are visible from Osturna and the village is situated at an altitude of 2500 feet. Most homes are built on both sides of the dirt road.

Along the road are several small roadside church chapels for travelers. Each is eight foot square with a peaked roof with a cross on top. Inside the unlocked door of one is an altar for travelers to pray, with candles and occasionally flowers, if in season. Another chapel has no door and a four foot high crucifix atop the altar. The road ends on the outskirts of town, becoming a path into the woods and up the mountain.

When the spring winds come from the mountains the fresh breeze brings the pleasing smell of the trees and flowers, refreshing the air, like a promise of better life ahead.

Planting time was a family affair. The children would often skip school to help. Mikel Vascura rode the plow behind two horses, as the children and his wife, Anna, would be behind planting seeds. Mikel and his neighbor Ian bought the plow together, and each provided one of the two horses it took to pull it. When Mikel finished with it, it would be Ian's turn. The plow had two metal wheels and three plows between them. A wood seat was on top of the center plow. Sitting on the seat weighted down the plow so it could cut through the soil. He would have never been able to afford the plow himself, but by splitting the cost with Ian and sharing his only horse, it became possible. They each had two oxen for breeding that they could use for the plow as well. With seven children and another due soon, he had plenty of help to do the planting, so he could give Ian his turn quicker. While the bigger children worked, the toddlers were left to play with straw toys on a blanket in the field.

Half of his thirty-six acres were crops. Ten acres were for grazing his one horse, two beef cattle, two milk cows, two oxen, three goats, and four sheep. Eight acres were orchards of apples, nuts, and a few weak grape vines. Mikel still owed money on 25 of the acres to the landowner, and some years could only pay the interest on the balance due. Mikel didn't worry about it, however. As long as he owed money, he was valuable to his debtors.

When a beef cattle had grown to full size, Mikel would walk it to the butcher who would keep half the beef in the bargain and prepare the rest for Mikel. He would give Mikel cash for the hide. Next, Mikel would trade part of his beef to a neighbor for a calf in return. The rest he would put in his smoke shed. Sometimes, he would have to sell some of the beef for cash. The oxen were bred and calves were fattened and sold when a year old.

Mikel would do the same butcher arrangement with his pigs. He usually kept 3 or 4 pigs in a pen between the house and barn. The barn door was usually kept open so the other animals could come in and out of the rain or snow. The barn had a hay loft. It was the boy's responsibility to keep the manure shoveled out of the barn. They used a wooden wheelbarrow to haul it out to a place in the field where it was composted with leaves or any dead plant material. Occasionally, they would go around the pasture to collect manure for the compost piles. It was also their job to spread the composted manure in the crop field after crops were harvested in the fall. When the snow started to melt as spring approached, Mikel would turn the soil with the plow a few weeks before planting.

They planted wheat, potatoes, cabbage, beets, cucumbers, and feed for the animals. Chickens had to be kept in a fenced area with a coop next to the barn as the farm bordered the Tatra forest, from where wolves and lynx would come to the farm for an easy meal. Mikel kept a shotgun on a high shelf in the barn in case any wild animals came within shooting distance. In the winter they would go into the forest to hunt bear, wolves, or lynx. The smoking shed was usually almost empty. He had the same arrangement with the butcher with wild animal meat.

During planting Anna and the girls would stop early so Anna could start supper. As toddlers the girls weren't much help and would usually just take a nap. Soon there would be another child, but there was no time for Anna to rest. On the way to the house she would stop at the smoking shed to check the smoldering fire, then she would stop at the cellar door at the corner of the house. Mikel had dug a cellar under part of the house and lined it with stone. In it they kept potatoes, cheese made by Anna, cabbage, beets, canned pickles, and occasionally beer or wine made by a neighbor. Any cash made by the sale of hides, meat, or crops, or work Mikel or the boys did for a neighbor, they would use to buy fabric and thread for Anna, to buy shoes, or pay debts. Anna looked forward to the day when the girls would be old enough to help more.

One time a few years back Mikel and several neighbors each bought shingles and helped each other replace their straw thatched roofs with them. Most houses in the village still had thatched roofs. A couple of years before that, they replaced their mud brick floors with wood ones. Being near the forest, they cut some trees and took the logs to the saw mill, which had a steam powered saw that could cut them into boards for a fee. The homes of Osturna were made of squared logs, with mud between the logs, on stone foundations.

Mikel Vascura's house was located near the main road of Osturna, as were most houses in the town. The family land and barn were all behind the house, which was typical of houses in Osturna in 1896. The main room had a table in the center with benches. More benches were against the front wall for any guests that might visit. On the left wall was a fireplace with a stone floor in front of it, where all cooking was done. On the back wall, was a table for food preparation and for buckets. One bucket was for washing dishes and another was for drinking water. Shelves above this area held dishes. On the right wall was the narrow, steep stairs to the loft. Under the stairs was the inside access to the cellar. The loft was where Mikel and Anna slept. The only place to stand in the loft was in the center because of the slant of the roof. Out the back door was the outhouse, well, smoke shed, barn, pigpen, and chicken coop.

Next to the fireplace was the doorway to the children's bedroom, where four bunk beds lined the walls. Shelves on the walls between beds held clothes. Shoes were an ongoing problem, as someone was always outgrowing theirs. Hand-me-downs took care of some problems, but Mikel was always in debt to the shoemaker. There was no difference between boys or girls shoes, as all were made of dark leather that came up above the ankle. Toddlers just went barefoot until they grew into the smallest hand-me-down shoes that fit.

Soon the problem of shoes would be partly solved as the two oldest boys, Ilko and Andreii, were talking about going to America soon and there would be two less mouths to feed. Unfortunately, it also meant two less workers for the farm. Anna was not happy about it, as she feared them leaving and never returning.

On the last day of planting everyone sat at the dinner table talking about Ilko and Andreii leaving. "Why don't you two just go to Poprad again and get a job there?" Anna asked the boys.

"Poprad would only be temporary like last year, mom," Ilko said. "Besides, my friend is working in Poprad and he wrote to his family that there were no more jobs right now. I can make more money in America. I can then save money, and come back and buy land. No girl is going to want to marry a farm hand. The Rusinko's son did that and came back and got some land and married the Korcak girl."

Just then a knock came at the door.

"It's never locked," Mikel yelled. It had no lock.

The neighbor Ian Smolenak came in. "Sorry to interrupt your dinner," he said. "Did you finish planting today?"

"Yes I did," Mikel answered, relieved that they had finished. "I'll have one of the boys bring the plow and horses over to your place tomorrow after church."

"Good, I can get started Monday morning," Ian explained. "I could use Ilko and Andreii to help. Only a few days. That's all I can afford."

"Yes, sir. We will be there," Ilko said. "What's that you got there?" referring to the magazine Ian had in his hand.

"My son James was just here visiting and gave me this magazine to show you Ilko," Ian pointed out. "It has an article he thought you might want to read. He knew you were interested in going to America."

"Yes I am," Ilko said, excited. "Thank you. I'll return it when I am finished." The magazine called Obzor, published in Skolica, was open to an article written by a Slovak man named Sustels, who immigrated to America and wrote about his experience.

"I'll let you read this article when I'm finished," Ilko said to Andreii. The article gave information and advice on traveling to America, locating employment, wage ranges, and engaging in business with Americans. It told about agents representing industrial and mining companies in America, and how they were recruiting Slovaks and Rusyn to work in there. The agents also working with steamship companies. The article warned not to sign a contract as they were not legal in America anymore. Furthermore, the article said that the immigrants will see recruiters when they go get passage on ships in Hamburg or Breman, Germany, the departing point for immigration from Eastern Europe.

It took the boys all evening to read the article. They didn't have that many years of education and often they missed school during planting time and harvest times. Reading the article meant reading by committee, as the children helped each other sound out words they weren't familiar with. The article advised that anyone who expected to have no money when they arrived in America, needed to have the information of who was going to meet them, and the person's address, and where they planned to work. If the immigrant had no money, no job waiting, or no relative waiting to offer financial support, the officials would not let them enter the country.

On Sundays after the cows and goats were milked and animals fed, everyone dressed for church. The Vascura children all had dark hair, brown eyes, and prominent eastern European noses. No more work would be done for the rest of the day. They had special clothes worn on Sunday, holidays, or special occasions only. The ladies' dresses were embroidered with designs on the skirts, blouses, sleeves, and hats. The men's shirts would be embroidered also, or they would wear an embroidered vest.

St Michaels the Archangel Greek Catholic (Ruthenian) Church, was a wood church with an onion shaped steeple. Its interior had many colorful paintings of Saints, with white walls and gold painted trim. It would have several masses each

Sunday, in order to handle all of the villagers. The Vascuras didn't live far from St Michaels Church, so they would walk to church early in order to watch all other villagers coming down the road. The women would look to see if anyone had a new dress, so they could admire the embroidery. The boys would look at the notice board to see if a dance was planned soon, or talk to friends. This Sunday, Voytek saw something new on the notice board.

"Ilko, Andreii, look at this," Voytek yelled to his older brothers. "A priest who was in America will be at the church on Wednesday to speak about working in America. It says two o'clock at St Michaels."

"I'll definitely be there," Ilko said, anxious for as much immigration information as possible.

"Me, too," Andreii said. "We'll have to get the clock fixed."

At dinner that night they ate pyrohies, sauerkraut, red beets, and chicken, while everyone still wore their Sunday best. Anna wore a big embroidered apron only worn on Sundays when preparing Sunday dinner.

"Are you boys going to talk to the priest on Wednesday?" Mikel asked.

"Yes," Ilko and Andreii both said.

"Me, too," Voytek added.

"Son's, if I were you and young like you, I would be going to America myself," Mikel advised. "But I am old, married, have seven children and another on the way, and I have a farm to run. You have an opportunity. Go and earn your money and come back with it to buy land for yourself. Don't be in debt to everyone like I am. But promise me this, if you decide to stay in America, send a little money back for a brother or sister to go if they wish. You must promise to write every month."

"I promise," Ilko said.

"Me, too," Andreii agreed.

"Promise your mother you'll come back," Anna insisted.

"I promise," Ilko said.

"Me, too," Andreii agreed.

"The big question is, how much it will cost?" Voytek asked. "Hopefully we can find out from the priest."

The five boys went to the church on Wednesday. Ilko was 24, Andreii 19, Josef 17, Voytek 15, and Grigory 13, all strong from a youth of labor. Voytek seemed to be the most excited about the possibility of going to America.

"I want to make lots of money and owe no one," Voytek told the others as they walked to church. "I want to have two or three of everything. I don't want to sit in my underwear waiting for my clothes to dry. I don't want to wear the same Sunday clothes for the rest of my life."

Father Mudrak, St Michael's old priest with a long gray beard, introduced Father Volansky, a younger priest with a short black beard. "Father Volansky is from Pennsylvania, one of the states in the United States of America," Father Mudrak told those gathered. "He is here to visit family and we have asked him to talk about the journey to America and the work available there. Some people in the area have been going to America in the last ten years, and many more wanting to go."

"Despite what you may have heard, America is not paved in gold," Father Volansky started. "Most of the streets are not paved, just like here. Yes, you can earn more, but it will cost you more to live there. Yes, you can earn in one day what it will take you most of a week to earn here. But a room in a boarding house will cost you ten US dollars a month, which is fifty korunas. It will be more if you are married. If you have children you will need to rent an apartment. You pay by the week and you pay your week in advance."

"You need to take money with you," he continued. "The climate is similar to here, warm summers, cold winters. You need money for a train to get to Hamburg or Breman, Germany to travel on a steamship to America. The steamship will cost you twelve US dollars in steerage, which is an area low in the ship with many bunk beds. To get a second class cabin it is twenty US dollars more."

"When you get to America you must have money with you," he went on. "If you don't, you better have a relative to come get you. If you have no one to meet you, and no money, you won't be allowed in the country. After you process through the immigration center they will ferry you to the train terminal to take a train to where you are going. It is helpful to have the address of a friend, or relative, or place where you want to go to look for work, so that you know where to get your train ticket to."

"So before you plan to go, write to anyone you know and ask where they are hiring workers," he explained. "I have a parish in the coal mine area and they are hiring unskilled workers. It pays better than a lot of the factories, but it is hard, dirty, dangerous work. A lot of you will be able to save money to send home, but keep in mind there are strikes and layoffs, so save money for those times. If you want to go into farming in America you will need money for land and equipment. If you have a skill, you can make more money. But if your skill is farming, than you can work on a farm, or as an unskilled factory worker, or miner."

Ilko asked the priest what the total cost might be.

"If you go steerage, that's twelve US dollars and that includes your food, and you need about two dollars for the train to the ship," he answered. "You can take food on the train. When you get to America you will need train fare. If you are not going too far, then you will need about three dollars for fare and food. Plus you will need money to live your first week or so while finding a job. If you land in America with ten US dollars, that would be good. An American dollar is five Korunas. So before you leave home it is best to have over 100 Korunas per person."

On their way home the boys realized that they were in need of saving a lot of money. "One hundred Korunas each for me and Andreii," Ilko said. "That's a lot. Once we are there then you boys can come with less, because you can stay with Andreii and I when you get there."

"When we are over there, we can put our money together and start a business or farm and work for ourselves," Voytek said, excited about the dream of America, with no idea of how he would accomplish this.

"Or maybe even come back here and buy our farm or business," Andreii suggested.

"We got to get there first," Ilko reminded.

The next morning Voytek took the farm dog, a border-collie that lived in the barn and was never allowed in the house, out to the fields to chase birds and rodents from the fields so they wouldn't dig up the recently planted seeds. He went to the edge of the forest to find a stick to swing at any seed-eater he might see. He noticed the wildflowers starting to bloom, which meant that during the summer, he would be pulling weeds and wildflowers from the planted fields. Wildflowers in the pasture didn't matter as the cattle and sheep liked to eat the wildflowers.

The two oldest brothers were sent hiking to the Osturniansky Creek at dawn with fishing poles. The smoke shed was getting empty of fish, as it had been lent recently and their parents wanted fish for Friday and Saturday. There would be meat on Easter Sunday. The Creek ran near the town's main road, but for fishing you had to walk a couple kilometers to where it widened just before the river. The fishing was better there. Birds flew past Ilko, as he and Andreii sat on rocks next to the creek.

"I can't wait to go to America," Ilko said as he baited his hook. "Jobs are plenty. They have big factories. Money will be in our pockets. I will buy a suit, just like a gentleman."

"What if we don't like being in a factory all day among all those machines," Andreii commented as he tossed his line in the creek.

"Then we work somewhere else, or we come back with money in our pockets and buy some land south of here where it is not so hilly." A starling dug for a worm a few feet from Ilko, unconcerned about their presence.

"If the lordship landowner will sell to you, and at what price? At least here in the hills they don't control that much land." A stork swooped just over Andreii's head as it dove into the creek for a fish. "That would have been my fish," Andreii complained to the stork.

"That's the problem here. The poor man has no say. In America the poor man votes for the leaders and can buy land."

The swallows in the trees started to make a lot of noise alerting each other as an eagle soared high above.

"We will need to learn English in order to vote."

"Yes we will need to learn as quickly as possible, to help us at work, to read newspapers, and eventually to vote. If we don't try we will never know if we like it. We better do it now before we have a family."

At St Michael's Church, the ropes of the bells were tied on the Thursday before Easter so the bells could not be rung on Good Friday. They would be untied on Saturday.

Friday morning everyone gathered around the table. Anna had given a bowl to each. She put pin holes at opposite sides of each egg being sure to break the yolk with the pin, and handed it to each person who would then blow in one hole so the insides would come out the other hole and into the bowl. After two dozen eggs, a bowl in the center of the table was full of empty uncracked eggshells, while everyone's bowls were full of raw egg. Each bowl's contents were then dumped into a pot and stirred as milk was added. While cooking over the fire, Anna added salt, cinnamon, and sugar. After a few minutes a cheesecloth was placed in a bowl and the mixture was poured into this bowl. The cloth was then gathered together and tied at the top with twine. This then hung from a hook above a bucket to catch drips.

"Nobody touch the hrudka while it cools," Anna commanded. Her mother, being Slovak, had taught her how to make the Slovak Easter cheese.

Different colors of wax were melted and placed in separate bowls on the table. A pile of pencils, bird feathers, pins, and slivers of wood had been stacked on the table to use as brushes. Each child took whatever brush tool they wanted, dipped it in a color of wax, and started making designs on the empty egg shells, using different colors to create a uniquely designed kraslice egg. Further east in the Carpathians the eggs were sometimes called pysanky.

"Children, these eggs represent life." Anna reminded the children. "The color yellow represents light, like the sun. Blue represents water and green represents plants, like leaves and grass. Put your finished eggs in the center of the table to dry. We will need the rest of the table for baking. Did you boys finish fileting the fish you caught yesterday?"

"No, the fish are in the smokehouse," Andreii answered. "I'll finish fileting after I complete my second kraslice."

On Saturday morning, the boys took turns bringing buckets of water from the brook. It was a tradition on Easter Saturday to bathe in brook water instead of well water. The girls went first, heating the water in a kettle at the fireplace, and then Anna would pour it in the wash tub. The boys had to stay outside doing chores and fetching water, while the girls bathed. Then Mikel and the boys would go next, as Anna combed and braided the girls' hair in the bedroom. When bathing was done, Mikel and Ilko trimmed the boys' hair with scissors while they sat on a bench outside the back door.

Anna then started to make the items for the Easter basket to take to church. She cooked kielbasa, ham, bacon, and boiled eggs. While they cooked she made sweet bread with raisins and nuts on top. When finished, she put the items in a wicker basket along with cheese. She covered the items with a poscha, an embroidered cloth made for just this purpose. She then tied a candle to the side of the basket.

Before midnight the villagers went to church as the bells tolled, carrying their Easter baskets with them. In the church, the candles of the baskets were lit during the service, and the women walked to the altar for the priest to bless their baskets. At the end of the service, the villagers would walk out singing with the candles still lit. As they walked down the road, the singing continued until everyone was back in their homes. At home the basket was placed on the table with decorated eggs placed around it, and no one was to touch it until after Easter Sunday mass.

After church on Sunday, everyone ate heartily from the food that had been in the basket, plus more, including the hrudka. The children took the decorated eggs to show to friends and to look at their friends' eggs.

"The children are growing so fast," Mikel said to Anna as they sat on the bench in front of the house watching village children laughing and going from house to house to show their eggs.

"Aksinya and Marya are so cute," Anna observed proudly. "They are so proud of their eggs." Aksinya was 9 and Marya 4. "I'm glad Easter is over, this baby is coming any day now."

"I hope it is another girl," Mikel wished. "You could use the help in the kitchen. I'm sure, if it is a girl that she will be just as pretty as Aksinya and Marya. They are not only pretty, but smart too. Aksinya is reading so well. The priest said she was one of the smartest at the school for her young age."

"So true," Anna agreed. "Will there be any boys left for them to marry?"

"So many boys going to America with older brothers or parents."

"And haven't come back," Anna frowned. "They don't write either. Of course no one in town can write very well anyway. Ilko had his heart set on that Petras girl, but she went to America with her two brothers."

"Yes I remember. The family sold me some animals to raise the money. What was her name?"

"Helena," Anna answered.

"The children sent some money back and the Petras were able to replace some of those animals," Mikel pointed out.

"I think Ilko isn't looking to marry other girls, because he wants to go to America and find her."

"It's a big place to look for someone."

"The Petras said the children are in a place called Nujusy or something like that."

"I think Ilko and Andreii should have enough money to go after Christmas, or maybe after planting next spring."

"I'll miss them," Anna said as she massaged her pregnant stomach.

"With less mouths to feed, I can sell more crops and buy you and the girls some fabric to make clothes," Mikel said, putting his hand on her stomach. "You deserve it. And the boys can send some money, because Voytek is sounding interested in going too."

"It is so far away and they are so young," Anna complained.

"We were married and had a baby at Ilko's age," Mikel reminded.

"Yes, but we had our parents helping us build this house with logs cut from the forest, and they helped us by giving us some animals," Anna reminded him.

"There was some land available. Now the good land is all gone. The rest is too hilly and rocky. Also I have seven, soon to be eight children to feed. My wife makes healthy babies." He winked at Anna.

"I guess we have been blessed," she smiled. "And are about to be again. Go get the neighbor ladies. I have been having pains."

The ladies struggled to get Anna up the steep stairs to the loft. No doctor was anywhere near Osturna. Babies were delivered with the help of other mothers.

Early the next morning, a baby girl was born to the Vascura family. Mikel chose the name Anna for the baby's name to honor his wife. The baby would be called Annie.

Aksinya and Marya told their mother that they would help her take care of their baby sister. "She is better than a doll," Aksinya told her parents. "And prettier."

"But she will make messy diapers," Mikel warned. "Your doll doesn't."

The summer growing season went well. At harvest time Ian and Mikel worked out a deal with a landowner who had a large estate, to rent his reaper to speed up their harvest. They would first work for the landowner along with their sons to harvest his land. They would use their two horses and two of the landowner's horses, and when finished they would move over to their fields and use the reaper. It was much faster than by hand with a sickle, and would earn them some cash. Most villagers harvested wheat with their sickles.

After the harvest the girls and Anna worked on making Ilko and Andreii some new clothes and coats for their journey. The two soon-to-be travelers were getting excited about leaving after the spring planting.

Forty days of fasting with no meat or dairy preceded Christmas. The Christmas Eve Holy Supper started when the first star appeared on the sky on January 6. Before it got dark Mikel and the boys would take some apples, pears, cabbage, and potatoes and feed them to the animals as was the tradition on Christmas Eve – 'feed the animals from your table first.' They would then take some straw and place beneath the table, another tradition. A white cloth was laid on the table, and a large round loaf of bread with a candle in the center of it, was placed in the middle. Around the bread, nativity figures were placed. Another candle was placed in the window, and when stars came out, the candles were lit.

As they all sat around the table, Mikel gave each of them a wafer. Mikel then said a prayer for God's grace, after which, they each dipped their wafer in honey, and wished each other a joyful feast. It was an age-old custom that represented charity, unity, and friendship.

The food for supper had no meat, as this was the fortieth day of the fast. They ate well as they had bobalki dough balls with poppyseed and honey, pyrohy dumplings with just potatoes inside, sauerkraut, bean soup, apples, walnuts, and fish.

After supper Mikel read the nativity story from the Bible. A small tree was placed on the end of a bench so the children could put the decorated eggs from Easter on it as ornaments by putting a thread through the holes.

When carolers came down the road, the children joined them. "See you at church," Anna yelled to the children as they left singing.

Once they were gone, Mikel and Anna laid presents on each of the children's beds. On Ilko and Andreii's beds, she put new shirts and socks. On the girls' beds, she put new embroidered babushkas and straw dolls with little dresses. The other boys each got pants and socks. For weeks she had been hiding the items under her bed as she made them. The baby got booties.

An hour before midnight the church bells rang for the Christmas Eve service. After the service the children ran home to find their presents on their beds.

At midmorning on Christmas Day, the church bells rang for the Christmas morning service. Afterwards, a big lunch was prepared, followed by friends visiting. Midafternoon the church bells rang again for the Christmas afternoon service. Caroling followed after this service, with friends visiting each other's homes where food was on every table. Christmas day meals included meat and sometimes wine, beer, or brandy if the family had any.

That evening Anna announced to family and friends that she was expecting another child. Mikel turned red as the men visiting teased him that he was getting too old. Mikel knew that the year ahead would be different with another baby, and losing two of his sons to a land far away.

After the spring planting in May, Ilko and Andreii prepared to leave for America. They each rolled their clothes on a folded blanket, then tied a rope around it. This was their luggage. Like so many in Eastern Europe, the chance for better economic opportunities beckoned them to the faraway land. It was a land of no royalty, no monarchy, a land of choice, of private land ownership, and voting in elections.

After hugs and kisses, Anna and the girls were crying as the boys climbed into the small cart to leave. The younger boys wanted to cry, but knew it was not very manly to do so. The winds came from the mountains, bringing the pleasing smell of the trees and flowers, refreshing the air, like a promise of better life ahead.

Mikel drove the boys in his horse drawn cart through the mountains to a town in Poland where they could catch a train to Hamburg. In Hamburg they would get the steamship to America.

When Mikel got back to the house, three neighbor women came running out. Anna had given birth to another girl.

First, he and Anna thought they would never have a girl as they had five boys. Now they were just having girls, as this was the fourth in a row. But he hoped it would be the last. He was hoping that they would not be making the count even at five each in the future.

"Pop," Aksinya yelled as she ran out of the house. "Marya and I want to name the baby Ekaterina."

"Fine with me," Mikel agreed. "What did your mom say?"

"She likes it," Aksinya said. "Can we call her Kate for short?"

"Fine," Mikel answered smiling proudly at Aksinya's excitement. Aksinya was a big help to Anna. "How is mom doing?"

A neighbor woman came to the door and told him Anna was doing well and that she was nursing the baby, so he went quietly to check on her.

In a month the parents would take the baby to the priest to be baptized. Afterwards, the priest would fill out a baptismal certificate, which served as a birth certificate. The priest would then make a note in the church records. No copy would be sent to any town or district for record.

Chapter Two

Djurkans of Klemburk

Less than 100 miles southeast of Osturna was the village of Klemburk, about the same size, just under 2,000 people. Many sheep grazed the fields on low rolling hills where the Carpathian Mountains met the lower lands in the Black Mountain Valley. With few forests nearby, many homes were made of mud bricks with straw roofs. The mud bricks were one foot cubed and made by tamping mud in a wooden form with a heavy stone. The form was then turned over and emptied, allowing the mud brick to then dry in the sun next to a fire.

In the home's construction, the roof was framed and straw tied to it. Windows were few, usually one per side of the house, as glass was expensive. Looms to make carpets, blankets, or fabric for sweaters or coats, were in the corner of many homes. During winter or summer when planting or harvesting were not happening, there would be time for women to use their loom.

This area in the Presov region was part of the Aba's Lordship of Somos. The Aba's still owned most of the land.

Juraj and Ania Djurkan lived in Klemburk and worked for the Aba family estate by herding sheep and farming the land. The Djurkans, who lived in a small two room mud brick house on Aba land, were allowed to garden a half acre behind their home for themselves. On one side of the house, they had a fenced in area with chickens, and on the other side, they had a fenced in area with pigs. As soon as you stepped out the back door you stepped into the garden.

The estate was mostly pasture for sheep, with the remaining acreage reserved for orchards and crops. Juraj had two flutes he played when tending the sheep. When he played certain tunes the sheep would follow him. With the sheep dogs coming behind, he could move the sheep where he wanted. The flute he used the most was two feet long, called a koncovka with no finger holes on the side. You played it by placing a finger at the end and moving it to allow different airflow, thereby making different sounds. The other flute was five feet long, called a fujara, which made soothing sounds that relaxed the sheep. On Saturday nights, villagers would gather at the center of town for dancing. Juraj and others would bring their instruments, including a ninera, a viola with a keyboard, and a heligonka, a Slovak accordion.

The Djurkan home had a mud brick floor except for the stone hearth. In one corner of the main room, was Juraj and Ania's bed. The table and benches were in the center of the room. On the other side of the fireplace wall was a sleeping room for the five children and Ania's younger sister Marika.

31

The oldest children were girls, Dorotha, 15, and Elizabeth, 16, who would soon be of marrying age. Ania was concerned, as it seemed to her that many young men were heading off to America or another European city working the mills or mines. Few were staying to work at the farms. No one could blame them, however, since the estate farms did not pay well.

Ania was worried about her young sister, who was 25, eleven years younger than Ania, and not married. Ania knew of no young men Marika's age who were still not married. Ania's and Marika's parents were dead, and Ania wondered what would become of her. Every time Marika had her eye on a young man, he was off to somewhere else.

"I was talking to Aunt Karina," Marika told Ania one evening. "She said that cousin Gabriel wrote that he was working in the coal mines in a place called Shersvel or something like that. He writes that there are many unmarried men wanting wives, but few girls are there."

"That's where you need to be,"Ania said.

"That's what I was thinking," Marika agreed. "But I need money to go to America."

"You are good at sewing," Juraj added. "Why don't you see if you can make some clothes for people and earn some money? The butcher sure looks like he can use some new clothes. His wife doesn't sew well. Then you can save your money to go to America. But I wouldn't want you to go alone."

"Dorotha and Elizabeth said they would like to go also, if they can't find a husband," Marika pointed out.

"Not until they are both older," Ania said. "Besides it is going to take you almost two years to earn enough money or find husbands. Marika, call the children, supper is ready."

The three younger brothers complained about the same old food, "Pyrohy, sauerkraut, and mushroom soup," complained Jorge.

"I put cheese in the pyrohy," Ania said. "And put some beans in the soup."

"Good," he replied

"Let's say a prayer," Juraj said.

After Juraj said the prayer, Jorge asked, "Are we out of kielbasa again?"

"Yes," Ania answered. "But we don't have a pig big enough to take to the butcher, so you boys need to go fishing. Fasting time starts tomorrow anyway, so no more meat or cheese, or milk until Christmas day. So eat all these pyrohies."

"Gladly," Jorge said.

"Girls, do you think you would be interested in going to America someday with Marika?" Juraj asked Dorotha and Elizabeth.

"Sounds exciting," Dorotha answered enthusiastically. The petite Dorotha was always cheerful, and exuberant when taking part in the dancing and singing at festivals.

"We were just talking to Marika about it," Juraj said. "You all can get a job at a sewing factory, or as maids. It would pay better than here, I've heard."

"Or you could go to Presov or Bratslava, just as well," Ania suggested. "It is a lot closer. America is so far and we would never see you again. But if you are closer, you can visit."

"Wherever the young men are," Elizabeth said, causing the girls to giggle.

"You girls need to find some local things you can do to earn money, and save it for wherever you plan to go," Juraj said. "Work for someone at planting or harvest time, or make and sell clothes like Marika wants to do."

"We can do that too," Dorotha agreed.

"It is an adventure to go to a far off land," Juraj explained. "But it is for the young. I wish I would have gone to America when your mother and I were first married, but all I know is being a shepherd with a garden, working for the landlord, just like my father. I don't know what I could have done in America to support my family."

"You put food on the table, dear," Ania reassured him.

After church that following Sunday, Marika got some orders for her to make clothes. One woman wanted an embroidered dress made, and two other women wanted dresses embroidered. A man wanted her to make him an embroidered vest. Of course, she would have to work on them after doing her chores each day. But the chance for a dream of a better tomorrow makes the heart excited and the fingers move fast with delight. She had a plan and was determined to make it happen.

Marika's nieces were petite like her with brown hair that they kept covered with babushkas to keep the dirt off. With mud brick floors, sweeping was a daily task. The stone floor in front of the front door didn't keep the dirt outside, despite the family stomping their feet before entering. At the end of each day before supper, a washing of hands, arms, and face in a bucket of well water was a necessity. Saturday night baths in a round large tub were a welcome event.

A neighbor had a carpet loom that they would all use to make rag rugs to put in places around the floor. Old clothes became rags for the rugs. To rent some time on the loom women would give the neighbor some rags, food, or anything tradable that they would agree to.

Having mud brick walls, meant having pests in the walls. A stick was kept near the fireplace to swat at bugs. Crushed bugs would be tossed into the fire. Farm animals were always just outside the door, which meant plenty of manure to be shoveled into a small goat-pulled cart and stacked into drying piles out in the field and covered with plant material. Every few days it would be mixed with a pitchfork. When dry enough, the mixture would be packed into the same wood form used to make mud bricks. These dung bricks would be covered with straw to keep some of the rain out and on cold nights they would be burned in the fireplaces to save on firewood.

Parents knew that if they wanted a better life for their children, only change could make it better. The town had no doctor, just like Osturna. School was not formal, but a priest did the best he could to teach reading and arithmetic.

The Greek Catholic Ruthenian Church in town was named the Church of the Holy Virgin. The services were in Church Slavonic and everyone in town went to the church despite the town being a mix of Rusyn and Slovak. Rusyn was close enough to Slovak, as in some Slavic words the emphasis was just on a different syllable. The local Rusyn spoke with many Slovak words and visa-versa. The Djurkans were Slovak.

The bells of the church were different sizes producing different sounds, making a musical rhythm that Ania would often sing to. She would sing a made-up song to the children's delight. The sounds of the bells echoed along the rolling land to alert the shepherds that it was time for a church service.

The poor villagers shared a few shotguns for hunting. Being a farming area, the villagers had to hike to a preferred wooded area that had enough wildlife. The hike would take over two hours, so they would spend just as much time hiking to and from it, as they did hunting. The need for meat to feed their families was most during the winter when vegetables were limited. The hunting trips was usually hiked through snow and cold weather. Since the shepherd didn't own the sheep, he would have to buy one from the estate so he could butcher one for his family. Some days in late winter all they would have was eggs for breakfast, potato and cheese sandwiches for lunch, and pyrohies for supper. A four-mile fishing trip to the Hornad River would sometimes result in some trout. Many a Sunday after church found Juraj and some neighbors heading to the river to try their luck at trout fishing to help fill the dinner table.

As the girls saved money, they looked forward to the trip to America. Dorotha and Elizabeth would work occasionally at the Abas' estate when they were having a special event, and needed extra maids or servers. The girls imagined Americans being rich like the Aba family. They dreamed of meeting handsome fellow immigrants in America who had high paying jobs.

"I'm going to meet a strong handsome young man with money in his pockets," Dorotha told her sister and aunt.

"I'll be happy if he has a jingle in his pocket," Elizabeth said.

"I'll be happy for a man, period, jingle or no jingle, handsome or not," Marika said being realistic. "He just has to have a good job so we can have a nice place to live."

37

Like many young Eastern Europeans, the girls were looking forward to a day when life might be a little better. Maybe have a home where the roof didn't leak; maybe have a home with a wood floor; maybe earn enough so you didn't have to raise smelly pigs; maybe have store-bought dresses. Everyone had their own idea of what they wanted to achieve by going to a land far away.

Chapter Three

Rusyn

Rusyn is an ethnic group who speak an eastern Slavic language. Rusyns are sometimes referred to as Carpatho-Rusyn, or Ruthenian, or Ruthenes. The Rusyn language is similar to Slovak or Ukraine, and even some Russian.

Around the year 900, people calling themselves Rus settled the Carpathian Mountains. They came from the nearby medieval Kievan Rus Kingdom. In these mountains they farmed for the next 1,000 years. Villages were small and poor. There were over a thousand Rusyn villages in the Carpathian Mountains in southeast Poland, northeast Slovak area, and western Ukraine area.   Osturna was the western most Rusyn village, literally, at the end of the road. At the end of the road a path went into the forest and up the High Tatra Mountains. These Rusyn families marked time by the harvests and the feast days of the saints. For them the world was unchanging, affixed to a permanent cycle and unaffected by the passage of time or kings.

The Slovak area was ruled by the Hapsburg Empire, where Hungarian nobles owned most of the land they ruled. Serfdom became abolished in 1848, but the nobles still owned most land. In the mountains the Rusyn could farm on land not claimed by nobles.

In 1867 a union was formed by the Empire of Austria and the Kingdom of Hungary creating the Austro-Hungarian Empire. The Empire now included the Czech and Slovak areas, Austria, Hungary, and the lower Slavic states. In the Slovak area the rulers made Magyar (Hungarian) the official language and wanted the schools taught in Hungarian, much to the dislike of the Slovaks and Rusyn. In the mostly isolated Rusyn villages, this was ignored.

Many Rusyns immigrated to the US in the 1880s and 1890s, settling in New Jersey, Pennsylvania, Ohio, Chicago, and Detroit. Immigration officials categorized immigrants by what country they came from. So, Slovaks were listed as coming from Austria or Hungary. Immigrants from the Ukraine area were listed as Russian because Ukraine was part of Czarist Russia at that time. A Rusyn person could be listed as Austrian, Hungarian, Russian, or Polish.

In 1054 the Roman Catholic church (Latin-Rite) and the Eastern Byzantine-Rite Churches in Constantinople split over differences, such as language; Roman services being done in Latin; and Eastern services in Slavonic or Greek. The Pope was the leader of the western churches and the Orthodox Patriarch was leader of the eastern churches. The eastern churches are either Eastern Orthodox or Greek Catholic.

St Michaels of Osturna was Ruthenian Greek Catholic as was the Church of the Holy Virgin in Klemburk. The Eastern Orthodox and Greek Catholic priests are married as the Roman Catholic priests are not. One exception is if the byzantine-rite priest is not married when ordained, he thereafter cannot marry.

Rusyn were friendly people who loved to dance and sing. Holidays and weddings were an excuse to bring out their instruments, which were usually passed down through the generations. Their instruments usually included a heligonka, a small accordion; the fujara, a long flute; a cimbalom, a box with strings across struck with a wood baton; the koncovka, a small flute; and the ninera, a viola with a keyboard. Songs were sung about their mountains, forests, family, and church. Special ethnic foods were always part of every special occasion, often made using doe, cabbage, homemade cheese, and pork sausage.

The Rusyn had songs and dances for every occasion, such as weddings and christenings, and were often spiritual in nature, especially for religious holidays. Songs and dances were taught at schools. Some dances were performed by couples and some by just men or women. Villagers dressed in colorful embroidered costumes for the occasions.

The Rusyn polka was popular among couples as well as the chirjana dance which is a flirtatious trio's dance in which partners switch places in order to meet a new partner. The khorovod dance was a women's circle dance done to greet spring or celebrate the harvest. The vechurka is a women's dance that features stamps, steps, and spins. The men's dances were more acrobatic. The gymnastic shepherds stick dance was performed at Christmas to honor the Christ child. The bear dance was a sportive and acrobatic dance in which dancers execute steps mimicking the Carpathian Mountain bear. The chapash men's dance uses rhythmic claps, kicks, slaps and hops. These dances would be accompanied with music and singing.

The women spent hours embroidering designs on dresses, shirts, and vests. Men and women only wore these embroidered clothes for special occasions or Sunday church. Being poor, a person may have only one of the dress, shirt, or vest. It may be their only one for decades.

Small villages could not afford a school or a teacher's salary, so the village would rely on priests and or parents. When a child turned six they went to church for school in the morning after chores. The children did not go to school during planting or harvest time. When they turned twelve usually they no longer went to school. The bible was used to help children learn to read.

The Carpatho-Rusyn language had several dialects. In Southeast Poland and some villages in the Slovakia area like

Osturna, the Lemko dialect was spoken. The villagers would also use Polish or Slovak words depending on what their neighboring villages spoke. Other dialects were spoken in other areas in Ukraine, the Presov section of the Slovakia area, northern Romania, northwest Serbia, and eastern Croatia.

Chapter Four

Going to America

One day just after Christmas in January 1899 Anna came running out to the field yelling to Voytek, "Come quick. A letter came from your brothers, we want you to read it." They had had little snow so far this winter and he was sending the animals out to pasture in the midday sun.

Voytek was the best reader in the family and the only one to have gone to the fifth grade so far. It was only the second letter from Ilko and Andrew, as Andreii now signed the letter.

In their first letter they told of sea sickness on the ship, then of the processing through Ellis Island. After the processing, they were put on a ferry to the train station on the nearby New Jersey shore. They could not take a train too far for they had little money. A Jewish man they met in steerage, had relatives who worked at one of the textile mills in New Jersey. He told them that the mills were looking for more workers. It was only twenty miles away, so they decided to go with the man and try getting a job there first.

They got hired two days later and got a room in a rooming house that had other Rusyn in it. In that first letter, they also wrote that while they were waiting for the right train at the terminal that night, they saw the main building on Ellis Island on fire. Flames leaped high into the night sky as the building burned to the ground. They could see people running to other parts of the island. Files of records were completely destroyed.

"They say merry Christmas," Voytek said to everyone as he read the new letter. "Ilko got married!" he exclaimed. "Ilko ran into Helen Petras' brother and found out that Helen was not married. After a few weeks of visiting each other on Sundays, they got married by a priest. Andrew was the best man."

"Oh, I'm so happy for him," Anna exclaimed with delight.

"They are expecting a baby in four months," Voytek read. The girls and Anna screamed in delight, with Marya jumping around and clapping her hands.

"A grandchild," Mikel said with a smile. "That calls for a drink of brandy."

"And Andrew has got a girlfriend," Votek read.

"Who is Andrew?" Mikel questioned.

"Andreii, he goes by Andrew now," Voytek answered.

"Oh, I forgot," Mikel said. "I hope he gets married too."

"Voytek and I want to go to America now," Josef said. "We almost have enough money. I'm twenty now. Time to go and see if I like it."

"I guess you are right," Mikel agreed. "Try it now while you are young and single. You can always come back if you don't like it, or want to come back and buy land."

"I'll soon be eighteen, I want to go with him," Voytek added.

"I would prefer you two not go alone, rather together," Mikel said.

"We can help with planting in March and then leave in April," Voytek suggested. He had grown into a strong young man. Now just under six feet tall, with wavy black hair and the start of a mustache under his big, broad, long nose. He looked the most like his father; broad strong shoulders and big biceps of a man of labor.

"Now then, let us write a letter to send back to them, and we will tell them to expect you in a few months," Mikel instructed, happy for his sons, but sad to lose two more sons. "Hopefully the letter will get there before you do."

The boys kept their word and helped with the planting. During the winter, Anna had made the boys new trousers and shirts. New shoes had been ordered from the shoemaker.

46

Their old coats would have to do. She also made some baby clothes for them to take to Ilko.

At dawn on the day to depart, they wrapped their clothes and the baby clothes in two blankets; rolled each, and tied each with ropes. Then they tied the ropes together to form handles. Also put inside each blanket roll was a sausage, brick of cheese, and loaf of bread. Mikel hooked up the cart to a horse as he had done two years earlier.

"I'm not going to cry," Anna said to her boys. "It was just yesterday when you two were boys." Tears came down her cheeks as she hugged each of them. "Write more than your brothers."

"I promise," Voytek said.

As the winds came from the mountains and chilled the tears on their cheeks, the fresh spring breeze brought the pleasing smell of the trees and flowers, refreshing the air, like a promise of better life ahead.

They rode the cart through the pass between two peaks, to the town in Poland where they would wait for the train going to Hamburg, Germany. After arriving at the train station, they ate some apples, pickles, and bread rolls that Anna had put in a cloth bag for the three of them to eat while waiting for the train.

"We will say a prayer for you tonight, boys," Mikel said as he prepared to go back to the cart. "God bless." They hugged, then Mikel hurried to the cart so the boys wouldn't see his tears.

Their train left late in the afternoon and after changing trains twice, they arrived in the next morning in Hamburg. It was a short walk from the Hamburg train station to the building next to the river and docks, where they bought their tickets for America. When they went to the clerk to buy the tickets, they were asked if they were immigrating, then sent to a desk where a man filled out a form for each. They were asked name; marital status; occupation; could they read, if so what language; what nationality; address just left; final destination in the United States; after buying the $12 US passage, how much would they have left; if joining a relative, what is their address; ever in prison; condition of health; and crippled or not. Fortunately the man knew some Rusyn so they were able to understand him. The boys could see that the form was in German and English. When the boys told him their town and Austro-Hungary, he asked if they spoke Austrian or Hungarian.

"No," they answered.

"Most people we get here from Austro-Hungary don't," he said in Rusyn with a German accent. He asked if they wanted to upgrade from steerage to second class for only 100 Korunas more.

"No," they answered.

"I guess not, since you each said you only have 40 more korunas each after paying for your ticket," the official said.

"But I have to ask. The ship leaves in two days, the 13th. Report to that ship you see over there." He pointed behind them, where through the window, they saw a large ocean going steamship. They couldn't imagine how such a large ship could move in water, or not sink.

He gave them each a ticket and an inspection card with all the information on it that he had just asked them. "Keep these with you at all times," he instructed. "Do not sleep in the waiting room here the next two nights. There are rooming houses and hotels down the street. Be here by eight a.m. sharp on the 13th."

They grabbed their bundles and walked down the street wondering what to do for the next day and a half. "We don't have enough money to spare for a room," Josef said. "Maybe we can walk out of town and sleep in a field under a tree."

"I got an idea," Voytek suggested. "See all those boxcars over in the train yard? Let's look for some empty ones not near the street."

They found an empty one that was open and not near the street. "We can sleep in here tonight and just walk around the city during the day," Voytek offered.

"Good idea," Josef agreed.

When the sun was coming up on the 13th the boys felt the box car jolt and start moving, waking them quickly. They jumped up, gathered there belongings, and jumped off the boxcar as it was moving. They walked to the ship where a line had already formed at the ramp. Promptly at eight a.m. the officials started checking the passenger tickets.

Upon entry, at the top of the long ramp, the boys were on deck and then directed to a stairway to the next lower level, where another man checked their ticket and directed them to continue down to the next level. There another man checked the tickets and directed them again down to another level.

"If we go any lower we will be at the bottom of the sea," Voytek commented.

There were no more stairs and yet another man directed them to a large room. Inside another uniformed man motioned them to bunks, then motioned them to place their bundles on each bunk. The room had dozens of bunks lined up with just a couple of feet between each of them. On each bunk was a straw mattress, a blanket, a tin cup, tin plate, and a knife, fork, and spoon. Along the one wall was long tables with benches. Only men were assigned to this room.

Within an hour the room was full and a man in a white coat came in and told everyone to line up next to the tables with their tickets and inspection cards. Speaking in a type of Slavic with a German accent, he looked into their eyes and carefully at their scalp and hands. He had them lift their shirts and felt their foreheads for possible fever. He asked each if they had any disease or ailments. After passing someone, he would stamp the ticket and inspection card. He would place some check marks and initials on the card and hand the ticket and card back to the passenger.

In less than two hours, all had had their health inspections and the ship doctor was on his way to another steerage room. Just after noon, a man rolled a cart into the room. Passengers grabbed their utensils, plate, and cup and walked over to the man to get stew, bread and butter, and tea. Everyone sat at the tables to eat.

A restroom was next to the room and passengers rinsed off their eating items in sinks and took them back to their bunks. The room had several sinks and toilets and a long trough for urinating just like the one at the train station. These were the first toilets the boys had ever seen. They were amazed at the handle on the sink where you could turn it and water flowed, no pumping a handle to get water from the well like at some of Osturna's homes. Their home had no pump, just boy power to go to the well with a bucket.

Just then the ship whistle sounded and bells rang. They could feel the ship start to move. "Let's go upstairs and watch," Voytek said excitedly.

As they walked through the steerage level, they could see two more large rooms, one with men and one with women. Past those were many small rooms with families with children. On the deck they could see tug boats pulling the ship to the center of the Elbe River. Passengers on deck were waving at people on the docks, who were waving back. The ship slowly steamed its way down the river until it headed into the North Sea. From the deck they could see the cities along the river with their many buildings. They were in awe at the size and sheer amount of them.

They stayed on deck until supper time which was 6:00pm for their steerage room. With no watch, they would have to ask someone every few minutes. In Osturna you didn't need to know what time it was. The church bells rang when it was time for church service or for school to start. Everything else was done by the sun in Osturna. For supper they had meat, potatoes, bread and tea. With nothing to do, they wandered about the ship, only to find there were parts of the ship they weren't allowed to go through. Evidently first class passengers don't associate with steerage. At dark they went back to their bunks. They used their bundles as pillows, and put their coats and boots at the foot of their bunk.

At 8:00 the next morning they had oatmeal, bread, and coffee. They then went to the deck to see what could be seen. At the front of the ship they could see land in the distance on both sides of the ship.

"Where are we?" Voytek asked Josef.

"I don't know," Josef said.

A nearby passenger understood them and answered in Slovak. "In the English Channel," the tall man with a hat informed them. "England to the right and France to the left."

"Oh my," Voyteck said. "Thank you."

"We'll soon be in the Atlantic Ocean and no more land for the next seven days," the man continued. "Then you'll start to see America."

"I can't wait," Voytek exclaimed.

"Where in America are you headed?" the man asked.

"Nujuzy," Josef mispronounced.

"New Jersey," the man corrected. "Good luck finding a job there. There, and New York are the first places everybody goes. I'm going to meet my brother in Chicago."

"We're going to meet our brothers in New Jersey," Josef said.

"Where's Chicago?" Voytek asked.

"An almost two day train ride from New York," he answered. "I'm Vasko Ruznaryk."

"I'm Voytek Vascura, and this is my brother Josef."

"I'm thinking of Americanizing my name to Vance," Vasko said as he looked at a small book. "This is a book of English baby names. I'm starting over. No longer a farmer. I will work at something else."

"Where are you from?" Josef asked.

"Near Presov," he said. "How about you?"

"Osturna, a village near the High Tatras," Josef answered.

"Can I see that book?" Voytek asked.

"Sure," Vasko offered. "Let me know when you're done with it. I have to give it back to the man I borrowed it from."

Voytek sat on a bench while looking at the book. It wasn't easy, even though he had learned both the Roman alphabet as well as Cyrillic, he did not know English. After a while, Voytek announced to Josef that he had decided to use Walter Wascura. He had decided that W sounded more American for their last name, and he liked the looks of Walter for his first name.

The next day while they were in steerage eating lunch, a 14 year old boy named Dimitri from a Rusyn town in Poland, was asking them how much train tickets cost in America.

"Why, how much money do you have?" Vasko asked.

"I have only one ruble and 9 kopeck," Dimitri answered.

"That's not even one American dollar," Vasko said. "Where are you going?"

Dimitri showed them his sign he had with his sister's Ohio address.

"Ohio is far, that is not enough," Vasko said. "You can't get into America unless you have at least two American dollars on you or someone to meet you. You can telegram someone

54

that you arrived, but it will take a day train trip for them to get to you. They will then have to pay two fares to get you and them to Ohio. Let me go get my map of the United States and show you how big it is and where you are going."

When he came back to the table, Vasko spread out the map on the table. "Here is New York City," Vasko pointed. "And here is Ohio. And here is Chicago."

"My sister doesn't have much money," Dimitri said.

"Where are you two going?" Vasko asked Josef and Voytek.

"Twenty five miles from the train terminal," Voytek said. "How far is a mile?"

"Six miles equals 10 km," he informed. "Say, about 40 km. Should be a cheap ticket. Do you boys have two dollars each or is your relative meeting you?"

"We have the money," Voytek said.

Dimitri looked frightened. "What am going to do?"

"Let me think," Vasko said. "Here's an idea. Let us go through the gate first. After we go through, you come to that side of the gate and we will pass $2 to through you. Then, you go to do your processing and you will be put through. We will be waiting for you. My brother wrote me that they did that too and it worked. You just give it back to us, but you are on your own after that."

"That might work," Dimitri agreed feeling better. "Let's try it. Thank you so much."

"Sounds good," Voytek agreed.

As they finished their lunch, a crewman announced in hard to understand Slavic, that all were to stay there, as a doctor and nurse were coming to give them vaccinations. "Have your ticket and inspection card in your hand," the crewman said. Everyone moaned.

That evening the ship began to tilt back and forth and up and down. The wind and rain was so bad that no one was allowed to be on deck. They were glad that the bunks were bolted down to the floor as everyone held on to them tightly.

That night few people slept. A line formed at their steerage room's restroom. Normally, if one was seasick they were told to go up on deck. But, with the storm, being on deck was too dangerous. Some passengers skipped the next couple of meals for fear of not being able to keep it down.

After the ocean calmed, Vasko said he needed a stiff drink after that the wild ride. "I wish we can get into the saloon," he said. "Steerage isn't allowed up there. Besides none of us have any money."

"I've never seen a saloon," Voytek commented. "What does it look like?"

"Let's go look," Vasko dared. "We'll have to sneak up. It's dark now, so let's go now." Several others followed them out of steerage. When no crewman was near, they lifted the bar meant to stop them, and climbed the stairs.

They reached that part of the upper deck allotted to second class. They heard a piano playing and a woman singing. "It must be that way," someone whispered and headed to the music. They looked in through open portholes at a plush saloon full of well-dressed passengers drinking from glass goblets and listening to the entertainment. Their look was a short one, as a crewman discovered them. He knew by their clothes that they were from steerage and sent them shamefully back to their own pen.

The days grew boring and steerage started to take on its own rank odor. Those that showered didn't have many changes of clothes, so they would put the same smelly clothes back on. Many, like the boys, had never seen a shower before.

Flirting with girls while on deck became a pastime of the younger men. The men weren't allowed in the women's steerage, so they had to wait for some girls to walk about the deck.

On the eighth day those on deck saw another steamship on the horizon heading west as well. It appeared that they were gaining on the other ship, so everyone got excited that they may pass it before the day was over. It was like a slow motion race. Bets were placed among some passengers with change to spare, as to how long it would take. After supper the other ship was finally being passed as everyone cheered. They were all glad to break the boredom. It was Voytek's 18th birthday and a way to celebrate it.

On the evening of the ninth day, a crewman informed everyone that land will be sighted at daybreak. If anyone wanted a spot on deck to see land, they better be on deck before sunup. Josef and Voytek were so excited they could hardly sleep.

Just before dawn, the Vascura boys were on the front of the deck, with their eyes focused west. "What is that light ahead?" Voytek asked anyone who might know the answer.

"That is Sandy Hook Lighthouse," a man yelled. "We will pass it on the right. New Jersey will be on the left and New York on the right." Voytek did not know what language the man spoke, but he made out a few words, as Vasko had been teaching them what little English words he knew.

As they got closer, the sun started to rise behind them. They could see the Lighthouse coming into view. The lighthouse was built by the British when New Jersey was a colony. Built of brick, the very thick walls had been built to last for centuries. Small twin lighthouses could be seen further to the south atop a hill. The New York harbor came into view as the ship slowed and tug boats came out to meet it.

"There it is," someone yelled. "The Statue of Liberty." Passengers started to point ahead to the left.

There, atop its pedestal, stood the largest statue anyone on the ship had ever seen. All were in awe at its size and symbolism of a robed lady holding a flame above her head. From the ground of Liberty Island to the top of the pedestal was over 150 feet, and from the top of the pedestal to the top of the flame was another 150 feet, making it over 300 feet high. From the deck of the ship it appeared to the passengers that they were almost at the level of the feet of the statue as they passed to the right of the statue, only a few hundred yards from it.

Voytek and Josef stood wide-eyed and open-mouthed in awe at the sight. They had been looking forward to this since their brothers had written home about it. They also could see Ellis Island with scaffolding around a huge stone building being constructed to replace the one that had burned down almost two years earlier.

With everyone looking to the left they hadn't noticed the docks coming up on their right. The tugs worked at positioning the ship beside a dock. The boys ran down to steerage to get their belongings. But steerage passengers were blocked from getting back up to deck. First class and second class would be processed first.

Finally, after noon, the steerage passengers were escorted to the gangway, where they waited in line as the custom officials checked baggage and inspection cards. Then they were shown to a ferry, where they were packed in for a short trip to the barge office which was being used in place of

Ellis Island until the new building was completed. From the ferry they could see all the numerous buildings of New York. There seemed no end to all the buildings, no matter what direction they looked.

At the barge office, the immigrants were directed to areas divided by language. One sign said Slavic, Hungarian, Russian, and Polish. This had the longest line. The shortest line was the one with the sign that said English. At this station they would be looked at by medical personnel. Coats, sweaters, hats, and scarfs had to be removed so they could look at arms, hands, and scalps. Eyelids were pulled up to look for trachoma disease. Scalps were inspected for lice.

If medical personnel thought someone needed a more extensive exam, a letter was put on their back with chalk; such as an L for lame, H for heart, B for back, or just an X. These people were sent to another room. If they looked healthy, they went to an immigration official who would ask them questions, such as name, where from, etc., like the man had asked in Hamburg and written on their cards. With several Slavic languages and dialects the translators could not know them all and were often misunderstood by the immigrants. Officials would help each other try to translate by committee. The officials checked the immigrant's cards to see if the answers they asked matched, plus asked more questions. In addition to those questions, the officials would ask if the immigrant was an anarchist. The boys didn't know what that was, so they said no.

They were also asked if they were a polygamist. They didn't know what that was, so they said no.

Voytek took this opportunity to Americanize his name and told the man Walter Wascura. "I am Rusyn from Osturna, Austro-Hungary, but just put down Austria. We Rusyn don't like Hungarians. They wanted us to learn Hungarian in school." The man wrote Austro-Hungary anyway as nationality and Ruthenian as race.

When finished with Walter, the official said, "Now take your money over to the currency exchange to exchange it for US currency. Then you will go to the ticket office to get your train ticket. After that you will go through those gates over there and show that man this form. He will direct you to the ferry. Welcome to the United States of America."

As they waited to exchange money, Walter asked Josef "Why did that man ask if we were an antichrist?"

"I don't think that was what he was trying to say." Josef guessed. "I think he was trying to say anarchist. Which I don't know what is. So I guess 'no' is the right answer either way."

It was April 22, 1899, late in the afternoon, two days after Walter's 18th birthday. The long lines had taken most of the day. One fourth of the immigrants were getting more extensive physicals. Many of these would be rejected or go to the hospital ward to wait for their illness to finish. Rejected ones would be sent back at the expense of the steamship company. Others would wait for relatives to arrive and get them. Many men came first to America to get a job and save to get a rental home for his wife and children, then send them money to come over. Those going to New York or New England were sent to a nearby train station. Those going to New Jersey or west would be put on a ferry to the New Jersey train station across the bay near Ellis Island.

After exchanging his money Walter waved to the boy, Dimitri, who had finished his physical and was being questioned. Walter walked up to behind the boy and stood next to him and slipped two $1 bills into his pocket, just as the official asked him how much money he had. Dimitri pulled the two dollars and Polish coins out of his pocket to show him.

"That won't be enough to get you to Ohio," the official said.

As he had been coached by the others, he said "My sister is meeting me in the Fildelfa train station."

"I think you mean Philadelphia," the official corrected. "Are you sure?"

"Yes."

Walter waited with Josef by the gate to the ferry. When the boy joined them, he gave Walter back the two dollars. "Thank you."

"Here take these coins," Walter offered.

62

"Are you sure?" Dimitri asked. "These shiny ones look valuable."

"From what I understand, the shiny ones are only what they call pennies, and are not worth much," Walter explained. "Let's go."

Walter and Josef's tickets were for Paterson, New Jersey, a short distance from Ilko's home. At the train station, Dimitri put his sign with his sister's address back over his neck. Walter pulled out a pencil from his pocket and wrote Ilko's address on the back of Dimitri's sign.

"Write me at this address when you get to your sister's home," Walter explained. "We want to know that you got there fine. Also, if you can't get there, you can find us at this address."

"Thank you both," Dimitri said.

"Vasko said you might be able to sneak on the train," Walter reminded. "But you must stay away from the conductor who collects tickets by going from car to car."

"I remember what he said," Dimitri said.

The three of them looked at the information board to determine which train would be the right one for Dimitri to take to Cleveland, Ohio. Several trains were lined up at the large station.

"I think that one is the one you need," Walter told the boy as he pointed. "Ours is this one and it's leaving now. We got to go. Good luck."

"Thank you, and good luck to you too," Dimitri yelled to them. Dimitri hung around the train waiting for a chance to board when the conductor wouldn't see him. A black porter was helping passengers with their luggage. Dimitri had never seen a black man. The porter noticed the boy looking at him.

"You need any help son?" the porter asked.

Dimitri didn't understand him so he pointed to the sign on his necklace.

"Yes, this is the right train to go to Cleveland. Where is your ticket?" the porter asked pulling out a blank ticket from his pocket and pointing to it. "Ticket."

Dimitri sadly shook his head no.

The porter pointed to the ticket window and smiled.

Dimitri took his coins from his pocket and hung his head as he showed his coins to the porter.

"Just barely over a dollar's worth of change," the porter observed in a low voice. "Better keep that for food." The porter shook his head. "Not enough son. Follow me."

The porter pushed a handcart full of luggage and motioned for Dimitri to follow him. He stopped at the baggage car, where he passed luggage up to another porter, who stacked it on shelves inside. "Cassius, do me a favor and stack this boy behind some trunks, where no one can see him."

"You tryin' to get me in trouble, Lew," the older Cassius said in a hushed tone.

"I'll take the blame," Lew said, speaking softly. He looked up and down the platform, then motioned for Dimitri to climb in. Cassius held out his hand and helped the boy up.

There he remained for several long hours. Later the next day Lew and Cassius told him when his stop was coming soon. When the train stopped, they opened the door and looked both ways down the platform, before motioning for him to jump out. On the depot, the sign said Cleveland, just like on his small sign on his neck.

He approached a man standing nearby and pointed to his sign, hoping for directions.

"Go down Adams," the man said as he pointed. "Then left at Hughes for ten blocks, then right on Williams for six blocks. You can catch a trolley at Hughes."

"Tank ya," Dimitri smiled, proud that he had remembered at least those English words to speak. He remembered the man saying Adams and Hughes and the direction he pointed, but understood little else.

When he got to Hughes, he found someone else to show his sign, and they also gave him directions. As he went further and after a couple more people giving directions, he

65

finally found himself in front of the address after two hours. The rooming house had the right numbers on it.

He walked up the steps and knocked on the door. A man yelled, "It's open."

Not understanding, he knocked again. A short man opened the door.

Dimitri pointed to his sister's name on his sign.

"You must be her brother," the man said. "Vasie, come talk to this boy. It is Hofia's little brother."

Vasie came to the door. "Welcome," he said in Polish, smiling. "Come in."

Vasie explained to Dimitri that his sister and her husband had moved to a farm about five miles away. "That is about eight kilometers. They are working there."

"Can you give me the address?" Dimitri asked.

"I don't know the address," Vasie said. "But, I can take you there. Let me get us something to eat first, before we go."

After they ate they set out to find the farm. Vasie paid for a trolley ride that got them over half way there, so it only took a little over an hour to get to the farm.

Hofia saw them walking down the road and started running to them. After a long hug, Hofia insisted that Vasie stay for dinner.

Walter and Josef's trip was much quicker, as they had taken the train only thirty miles. Following Ilko's instructions, they took a trolley from the depot, then walked the rest of the way. New electric street lights had been installed to their amazement. Despite the dark they could read the street signs because of the new electric lights.

When they found the boarding house, Josef knocked on the door. A tired looking old lady answered the door.

"We are looking for Ilko," Walter asked.

"Upstairs, third door on the right," The lady said in Ukrainian.

"Voytek, Josef," Ilko yelled when he answered the door. Embracing his two brothers, he said, "You two remember Helen, don't you?"

"Of course," Josef said. Helen was obviously in the last days of pregnancy.

"When is the baby due?" Walter asked.

"Any day now," Helen said as she tried to lean close enough to hug the boys. A basinet was in the corner, ready for use.

Andrew came running down the hall, having heard Ilko yelling. Soon a bottle of brandy was being shared as friends from the floor came over to meet the new arrivals.

Walter told them he Americanized his name to Walter and is spelling their last name with a W instead of a V. Andrew told them that he and Ilko were spelling their last name Westura, to sound more western. Andrew also announced that he and his girlfriend, Teresa, were getting married in two weeks. They toasted with the brandy again.

The next day the two younger brothers got a room in a nearby boarding house, then went looking for jobs. After a couple of days, they both found work at a textile factory, loading and unloading railcars and trucks. It was their muscular arms and shoulders that got them the job. Luckily for them the factory had someone there that knew Rusyn to help them fill out the forms which were in English.

On the day of Andrew's wedding, Walter was getting ready and combing his black wavy hair, when Ilko came into the room. "A letter came to my place today," he said. He handed him the envelope. Ilko looked very tired. The baby had arrived days ago and sleep was a rare thing with a new baby.

The letter was from Dimitri, telling him all about his adventure on the baggage car, and the kind black men who helped him. He wrote that he prayed the entire time he was in the baggage car. He was also grateful for the help of Voytek, the new Walter, and his brother Josef.

Walter told Ilko about the letter as they walked to the wedding, and said he would write Dimitri back. At the wedding, Walter danced every dance with any girl that would dance with him, especially the polka. Teresa and her friends had arranged for the use of the church's hall for the reception after the wedding mass. They invited anyone that had a musical instrument, with instructions to bring the instrument with them.

Chapter Five

Coal Mines

Walter, always positive and jovial, made friends easily. He was always hopeful for a brighter future. One of his friends at the textile mill was spoke frequently about the letters he got from a brother in Pennsylvania. The brother was making better money as a coal miner then they were making at the mill. His friend, Pete Shucosky, was wanting to join his brother and thought that Walter and another friend, Sam, would like to go with him. After a year in New Jersey at low wages, Walter felt he wasn't saving enough to get land back home, or get married and have a family if he stayed in America. It wasn't far to northeastern Pennsylvania, so he thought he would try it. He would like to make more money.

"I'm thinking of going to Pennsylvania with Pete and Sam to mine coal," Walter told Josef one day. "I could make more money."

"Yes, we aren't making much here, are we?" Josef said. "I have a chance with my friend Stephen to go to Chicago and work on the railroad. Same type of work, loading and unloading, but it pays more than the mills. Stephen says his cousin can get us a job."

"I guess that means we are both planning to leave here soon," Walter observed. "We'll have to tell Ilko and Andrew."

"True," Josef agreed. "Let's go talk to them."

A week and a half later after collecting their Friday pay which was always paid in cash, the four brothers went to the corner beer garden with the train schedule. They were planning each to leave with their friends the next morning; Walter with his two friends to Pennsylvania, and Josef with his friend to Chicago. After a few beers they all staggered back to the rooming houses, where Walter and Josef packed their blanket rolls for the morning. They still didn't have any luggage.

Saturday afternoon Walter, Pete, and Sam arrived in Wilkes-Barre, Pennsylvania. Josef and Stephen had taken a different train to Chicago. The three boys walked from the Wilkes-Barre train station down Market Street, where shops were busy with Saturday shoppers. Horses and buggies packed the street as street sweepers, with their shovel and brooms stuck in their barrels on wheels, looked for manure to scoop up. At the end of Market Street they crossed the bridge over the Susquehanna River into Kingston. Following Pete's brother's instructions in a letter, they turned right down Wyoming Avenue where more shops lined the street with just as many shoppers and buggies. After a few miles, they turned left on

Shoemaker where houses lined the street with children playing in the yards and people sitting on porches. They crossed the railroad tracks into the town of Swoyersville, where some of the houses were smaller than the ones they had seen in Kingston. Some were double blocks, as the local people called them, known as duplexes in New Jersey. After a couple of more turns, they came to a rooming house on Sidney Street near the corner of Kossack Street.

Pete asked the lady who answered the door at the rooming house, if his brother was home. "He'll be home later after his shift," she told them in Rusyn. "But he always goes to the beer garden down Kossack first. It's called Stanley's."

"Thank you ma'am," Pete said.

Heading down Kossack St, Walter could see the mountains ahead. As the winds came from the mountains, the fresh breeze brought the pleasing smell of the trees and flowers, like a promise of better life ahead.

They waited outside of the beer garden on a bench for Pete's brother to come by. They could see the large colliery at the end of Kossack Street. Miners headed down the street toward the colliery, as some came from the colliery covered in black coal dust. The tops of their heads were clear where their helmets had been, but their faces were black with coal dust. The whites of their eyes and the white of their teeth, contrasted brightly with the coal dust.

When Pete's brother saw the three young men sitting there with their blanket rolls at their feet, he started yelling in excitement, "Pete, you've come to buy me a beer."

"You bet," Pete yelled as he hugged him. He introduced his friends and they headed into the bar. It was a typical tavern in this working town. Located near the mines or factories, the beer gardens had living quarters above the taverns for the owner and his family. A long bar ran along one side with tables and chairs on the other side.

A beer or any drink was a necessary item for a miner when he got off work. His throat would be on fire from breathing coal dust all day, coating his throat and lungs. The beer washed down the dust from the throat. For a nickel a miner got a large mug of draft beer. The first one went down quickly, so the bartender put a second mug next to the miner quickly. Peanuts in bowls along the bar were free. A hungry miner could order a sandwich, but most had a wife waiting at home with supper, or lived in a boarding house where supper would be ready soon. Kegs were kept in the basement to keep cool with a hose running up to the controls. Occasionally the bartender would yell to his wife or a worker to run down to the cellar and move the hose to a fresh keg. "Running low," he would yell.

If the miner ran out of money when it got close to Friday payday, the owner would run a tab. On Fridays miners had to pay their tab. After a shift on Fridays, miner's wives would be seen coming into the tavern to snatch the pay money

73

out of their husbands pockets before they drank too much or started playing cards with their pay.

It was not uncommon to see a wife in babushka and apron, pulling her husband by the arm down the street with the husband still holding a mug of beer in his hand. When the bartender opened at noon the next day he would usually find one or two of his empty mugs left at his door by miners on their way to work at dawn.

On Sunday morning Pete's brother took the young men to church with him. At St Mary's Byzantine Church in Kingston, the service was conducted in Old Church Slavonic. Father Volansky gave the sermon. He was the priest who had spoken one evening three years earlier at St Michael's in Osturna about going to America. After the service, the priest stood outside on the sidewalk with his wife greeting parishioners as they left the church. Walter spoke to the priest telling him of their meeting three years earlier in Osturna.

"I remember your smile when we met," the priest said to Walter. "God bless you."

After church they walked to Wyoming Ave where most businesses were closed on Sundays. Only a couple of restaurants were open after twelve noon. Pete's brother knew of a sandwich shop open on Sunday afternoon.

"They serve hoagies here," he informed them. "And pyrohies and birch beer. It's not real beer. It is soda made from the sap of a birch tree. No alcoholic beer can be sold on Sunday."

"Birch tree?" Walter asked.

"That's the tree with white bark you see all over the wooded hills," he answered.

As they sat eating, Pete's brother John, gave them advice. "You boys are all over eighteen so you shouldn't have to start work as breaker boys. They only make fifty cents a day for pulling rocks and slate out of the coal. You can make over two dollars a day down in the mine if you are fast enough."

"Do they have openings for down in the mines?" Walter asked. "I want higher pay then what I have been making."

"Yes, if you look strong, they put you down in the mines," John said. "If you look weak, they start you in the breaker with the teenagers. But you boys all look strong and are over eighteen."

"We need miner clothes and what else?" Walter asked.

"You need clothes and boots," he informed. "They'll tell you to go to the company store and they'll take it out of your first pay. If you have the money go to Gantz on Main St. It's a clothing store and cleaners. They have the same stuff for less."

"I have enough, I think," Walter said. "I paid my first week room and board last night."

"You can get by with two shirts and two pants. You drop off the dirty ones before your shift, pick it up clean at the end of your shift," John suggested. "You can wear a set for three days. It'll really stink by the third day, though. We're lucky not to be in a mining town where you have to buy everything at the company store because there are no other stores. It's cheaper to live here with all the businesses, and with all the mines, the mine owners have to be somewhat fair. If they are not, the workers will go work somewhere else."

"What about tools and helmets," Pete asked.

"The mine supplies those. You pick up what you need each day before you get on the elevator," he told them. "Drop them off at the end of the shift for the next shift as you leave after your ten hours. When you sign up they will tell you all about it. They will tell you to go buy clothes at the company store, but if you have the money go to the Gantz store. You have to be strong enough to shovel coal into cars, or they will start you as a breaker boy."

"Are you in the union?" Pete asked.

"Yes. If anyone asks, tell them you are going to join as soon as you save for the dues," John said.

"What are dues?" Walter asked.

"For a strike fund," John answered. "If we go on strike, we have money to give members to pay their rent for a couple of weeks."

"Any chance of a strike soon?" Pete asked.

"There is some talk at some mines, but not at MacArthur Colliery," John guessed.

"How long have you been here?" Walter asked.

"A year now," he answered. "I almost have enough saved to get married. My girlfriend, Sofia, and I want to rent a house, but we need to save for furniture. We can rent a two bedroom house or a two bedroom double block for four or five dollars a month. We can rent out the other room to two of you boys for two dollars a week each, with two meals a day. Then we all can save. Since Sofia works at Gantz, we will have to help with the cooking."

"I can't cook," Pete objected.

"I know, but you can peel potatoes, slice meat, stir a pot," he suggested.

"True," Pete replied. After finishing their hoagies, they left to go meet Sofia.

The next morning, before six a.m., the boys walked to the mine with John. The closer they got to the MacArthur Colliery the more coal dust covered houses, the street, and mine buildings. Closer to the mine Kossack Street was no longer flat, but inclined to a hill where the colliery sat upon the hill, next to Main St. The colliery included the mine entrance, the large breaker that stood five stories high, and mine offices with coal dust covering everything.

John took them to the employment office. He introduced the three boys to the employment manager in broken English. The manger looked over the boys all standing almost six foot tall, with broad shoulders, no fat, just lean muscle.

"I like you Polkas and Russies," the manager said in English. "Big shoulders; bigger than some of the Welsh." The boys looked at John, not understanding.

"The boys no know much English," John said to the manager. "My brother Peter is Slovak like me. Walter is Rusyn. Sam is Czech. We all from Austro-Hungary."

"Slovak, Czech, Russie, Hungy, it's all the same to me," the manager commented. "It's all Eastern Europe. Looks like I'll have to help fill out the forms. We need more workers, so you're hired. John you stay to help translate."

The manager pointed to where they were to write their name. John translated. John told them the address of the rooming house. They needed to put down their date of birth and who to contact in case of emergency. Walter put down Ilko's address. They signed the form and gave it back to the manager.

"Nice hand writing, Walter Wascura," the manager complemented. "I'm going to put each of you with experienced miners. You get forty cents per five ton car you load. You get your helmet and tools before you go on the shaft elevator each day, and drop them off at the end of the day. You will be charged 25 cents per week for the tool sharpening. It comes out of your pay. Anything you buy at the company store which is next door, will be deducted from your pay. You will need the heavy duty clothes and boots like you see John wearing."

He waited for John to finish translating. "Get your stuff today" he continued. "You start tomorrow, day shift for training. Next week you will be on the evening shift. Do you have lunch pails?"

John asked the boys then replied, "Two do, one doesn't."

"You can get them at the company store," the manager continued. "We don't have a contract with a union, but we don't mind you boys joining the union. We know we pay better than most mines."

After the meeting, John headed to work, while the boys headed next door. Sam didn't have much money, so he bought clothes, boots, and a lunch pail to be charged to his first pay. Walter and Pete looked at the prices Sam was being charged and made a mental note. Then the three walked down Main St to the Gantz store. Sam's purchase was wrapped in brown paper and twine, and his boot laces were tied together and tossed over his shoulder.

At the store they saw Sofia, who was mending clothes at a sewing machine in the room behind the counter. She told the two girls at the counter that she could help the boys, as she knew what they wanted. She showed them the clothes they needed. "These are less than what he just paid," she said in Ukrainian. "We get these from the Maltby Mill here in Swoyersville. You'll save on the boots, as we get them from the boot factory in Scranton .The company store gets theirs from a supplier. Mr. Gantz saves by picking up his orders at the factories in his wagon. Be sure to save enough of your money for the next week and a half. You won't get paid until a week from Friday."

"I'll just borrow some from John," Pete said.

"He will charge you interest," Sofia joked.

Over half of the people in Wyoming Valley of northeastern Pennsylvania (Luzerne County) were employed in the mines. Mines were all over the valley, but most were on the west side of the Susquehanna River. Wilkes-Barre was on the east side and was the biggest town. One could stand on the bridge, turn in place, and count all the breakers as they were the tallest structures in the area. The west side of the river had many small towns that were made up of poor, Eastern European immigrant anthracite coal miners. Kingston and Forty Fort were the exception, as they had middle income residents; bankers, retailers, and professionals.

In smaller more isolated areas in West Virginia and Pennsylvania, the miners had no place to buy anything except at the company store owned by the mine owner, which charged inflated prices. The only homes to rent were company houses. On pay day the miner often just got an updated balance of how much he still owed the store. The miner purchased everything from the company store, groceries, clothes, and even rent. If the miner went on strike, he would be evicted out of his home that he rented from the mine.

The boys were now living in a larger area where there was competition among retailers, so they didn't have to buy from the company store. Some mines did have company houses to rent, but the miner had the choice of other places to rent not owned by mines.

The tall coal breakers were where the coal was broken into smaller sizes and rocks and slate were removed. After passing through the breaker, rocks and slate would be deposited into a culm dump, often called slag heaps by locals. The coal dust in these mountainous dumps became compressed and combustible, causing smoldering fires like flames escaping the depths of hell.

Breakers were located next to the mine entrance. Breaker boys would sit next to or over the conveyor belt and pull rocks and slate out as the coal moved by. Macarthur Colliery assigned those under eighteen as breaker boys. It would not hire anyone under thirteen. However, some mines would hire younger. An 1885 Pennsylvania law forbade employing anyone under the age of twelve, but was poorly enforced.

Before breakfast, on the boy's first day of work, everyone at the rooming house made their lunch at the kitchen table and paid a quarter for the lunch food. The boys sliced bread and ham to make sandwiches with mustard, and the cook gave them each a pickle. Then they poured coffee into their tin containers and placed them in their lunch pails.

At the dining room table the cook placed a bowl of scrambled eggs and a plate of bacon and biscuits. She didn't let anyone start eating breakfast until grace was said.

After getting their fill, the boys walked to work with John. The street was full of miners walking to work. Horse drawn wagons went up Kossack St as busses that anyone could ride. You just put a penny in a bucket next to the driver and sit on one of the benches on the wagon.

The ladies working at the Main St shops or in the mine offices would ride the penny wagon as it was called. Sofia rode it, as Gantz opened early and she was usually on the opening crew. Single miners would drop off dirty clothes for cleaning. Some boarding houses would do laundry for the same price. Some enterprising wives would take in laundry to do in their wooden wash tub, then hang out the laundry on the clothes line. In rainy weather Gantz would get more cleaning business, as they had a tumbling heat dryer which operated above a steam radiator heated by a coal furnace. It would dry the clothes quicker than the sun and breeze on a clothesline.

Each man was given a pick, shovel, and helmet and three candles as they walked to the elevator shaft. Men jammed into the 10 X 10 elevator. It did not go straight down, but went on a slight angle. As it came to each level, Walter noticed an electric light bulb next to the number of the level.

"You boys are working on level four today," John said.

"They have electricity in the mine," Walter observed.

"Yes," John said. "It's new. Only a few years now."

The mill where Walter had worked had electricity, but the rooming houses he lived at there and here did not. When they got to their level, John took them to the miners they would be working with. "Walter, this is Ivan. He is Rusyn also." John then took the others around a corner.

"What village you from?" Ivan asked Walter in Rusyn.

"Osturna," he answered.

"I'm from Lipany," Ivan told him. "You know your assigned number?"

"2115."

"Good, because we write our numbers on each car after we fill it. A man at the top writes down the numbers and we write the car numbers and our numbers on the card I have here. We turn it in at the end of the day. They make sure everything matches in the office. That is how you get paid. Now take one of the candles and light it off this candle on the wall and stick it on your helmet like this."

They then walked down a maze of tunnels where there was no more electricity, passing by a canary in a cage. "You have a canary down here," Walter observed.

"The canaries are our angels. If you ever see the canary dead, yell," Ivan instructed. "That means the methane gas is high and we have to get out of here. The canary is affected quicker than us or the mules."

Larger candles were on large beams the size of railroad ties, which were placed every so often to help support the tunnel. Mines had air shafts to draw air out of the mine and push air into the mine. This kept down the amount of methane gas. Most mines had one shaft for air in, and one shaft for air out. A few mines had only one shaft and these mines were susceptible to explosions, resulting in miner deaths. These gas explosions would start fires that could last years, resulting in closing off that section of the mine.

"We'll be working here," Ivan said as they reached the end of a tunnel. This end of the tunnel was only five feet high, causing them to bend over, their helmets scraping the top. Some areas of the mine were so low miners had to work on their knees until it was blasted larger. "Place your lunch pail over here next to mine." He took the large hand crank drill that he had been carrying and started drilling a hole. After making the hole about eight inches deep, he told Walter to drill the next hole while he looked for a coal cart.

84

When he returned he told Walter to drill another hole and pointed to the spot. Ivan used the pick to chip away at the coal seam on the wall. When Walter finished, Ivan put a stick of dynamite in each hole, then attached a fuse to each before attaching them together making a single long fuse. "When I light this, run and get down behind the cart," Ivan instructed Walter.

"Fuse lit," Ivan yelled loudly in English twice. Anyone in earshot stepped behind something and passed the message along.

The dynamite blew in sequence one after the other causing coal, rock, and slate to fly everywhere. A few conveniently landed in the coal cart. "Now, pick wherever you see a crack in the coal seam," Ivan instructed. After about a half hour of breaking coal off the wall with picks they were knee deep in coal.

"Time to start shoveling," Ivan announced. "We start around the coal cart and work our way to the wall. Be careful, rocks and slate don't go in. Toss them to the side wall. True it is hard to tell the difference in this low light. Just do your best." Large pieces of coal too big to shovel or lift would have to be broken up with a pick.

When the cart was full, Walter said, "I have to go to the outhouse."

"Go to the side wall and put your butt against the wall," Ivan instructed. "When you finish, put rocks on top of it. If you just have to pee, just do it on the wall."

"Need a mule here," Ivan yelled loudly in English.

"Need a mule to Ivan," someone yelled further up the mine. In a few minutes an old man came with a mule and hooked up the coal cart and took it away. Ivan marked their numbers on the cart and the cart number on the card he had pulled out of his pocket.

"What do we do if the mule drops manure?" Walter asked.

"Shovel it against the wall and cover it with rocks?" Ivan answered.

They shoveled more coal into a new cart. When no more coal lay on the floor, they went back to picking. After the coal seam got too smooth and hard to pick, they drilled more holes for dynamite. Around eleven o'clock they took a break to eat their lunch.

The mule drawn coal carts were hauled to a weighing station, then up to the surface in a separate shaft, where it was recorded and dumped on a conveyor belt driven by steam power. The coal went past the breaker boys, then ended up into railroad cars. Any rock or slate went onto the culm dump or slag heap as the locals called them. The slag could be sold for making of gravel roads. A full coal cart usually weighed about five tons and would pay the miners forty cents to split among the miners that filled them. If it was four and a half tons they would get 36 cents, five and a half tons they would get 44 cents, etc. If the cart had a lot of rock and slate in it, the scale man was to deduct weight.

On Walter's first day he made almost two dollars. It was almost forty percent more than he had made at the mill. "You did well on your first day," Ivan complemented. "Let me buy you a beer."

It was December 1900 when the ship arrived at New York Harbor from Hamburg with Dorotha Djurkan and her sister Elizabeth and her Aunt Marika. They hoped to be at their cousin's home by Christmas. The ship had arrived late in the day, so the girls had to wait until the next morning before they were put on the ferry to take them to Ellis Island. The new large stone building started operation earlier in the month. It was the largest building the girls had ever seen. Dorotha wore a babushka over her brown hair, her best embroidered dress, and a wool coat on this cold windy December day.

The girls went through the process without any problems. They used the last of their money for the train tickets to Wilkes-Barre, Pennsylvania. While waiting for the train, they ate the last of their cheese and sausage that they had in their bags. Ania had made the bags from carpets.

Many tears had been shed when Juraj and Ania took the girls to the train station in Presov in a borrowed horse and wagon to catch the train to Germany. Dorotha and Elizabeth looked to Marika for guidance, but she was just as frightened and nervous as the younger girls.

Now their second train trip headed over the forested Pocono Mountains to Wilkes-Barre. "Looks like the forests of Germany, only the mountains are not as high," Dorotha observed.

When they arrived Marika took out her letter from their cousin Gabriel with the instructions of how to find his house in Swoyersville. Carrying their heavy bags made the walk seem ever further than the four miles they walked in the dark. With the help of strangers they found their way.

Gabriel and his wife had rented half of a double block on Poland St. It had four rooms; an eat-in kitchen, a living room, and two bedrooms upstairs. The outhouse was in the backyard as it was for every house on this street.

It was late at night when they arrived. "Should we wake them?" Dorotha asked.

"Yes, I'm starving and thirsty," Marika said as she knocked on the door.

"Who is it?" a sleepy voice said in Slovak.

"Marika, Dorotha, Elizabeth," they all yelled.

Holding a kerosene lamp, Gabriel yelled, "Yukshamash," when he opened the door. "Cousins, come in." He placed the lantern down and hugged each girl. His wife came down and started making sandwiches after the introductions.

Eventually the conversation turned to where Gabriel might think the girls can get jobs. "Our next door neighbor works at the Maltby Mills," Gabriel told the girls. "She can take you there to the office and see if you can get a job there. They make clothes that miners wear to work, and also house dresses."

The girls slept on blankets in the baby's room that night. Gabriel planned to get three beds for the room and have the girls store their clothes under the beds. They would pay room and board to Gabriel, and help with the garden in the back yard in the spring. He would charge them a lot less than what they would pay at a boarding house. Most backyards in Swoyersville, even rentals, had a vegetable garden, an apple tree, and a chicken coop in the backyard, with the outhouse in the middle. Most of the immigrants had been farmers in the old country and were used to growing their own vegetables and caring for chickens.

Gabriel was looking forward to having his cousins staying there. They could use the extra money as they had another baby coming. He now had three more good cooks and help for the garden.

Two days later, a neighbor took the girls to the mill with her. The employment manager only had one opening, so he hired the oldest, Marika. He suggested Dorotha and Elizabeth try for a job at the Gantz store. "Ask for Mr Gantz," he told them in English. "They buy clothes from us and we are good friends. He's got two workers that are leaving to have babies. They work in his mending and cleaning department. Just show him the embroidery you did on your dresses. That will convince him. Plus, he likes pretty girls working at his store. The coal miners like to shop where there are pretty girls."

Dorotha and Elizabeth looked at Gabriel's neighbor as they didn't understand what he said. The neighbor translated and the girls did as he suggested.

At the Gantz store they were hired after mentioning that the Maltby Mill employment manager recommended the Gantz store as a nice place to work. Mr. Gantz had Sofia translate. It didn't pay much, mending and washing clothes, but no jobs for young unskilled immigrant women paid well, especially with little knowledge of the English language.

On the girls first payday, they gave Gabriel room and board and he went out and bought the three beds, mattresses, and sheets with the money from the girls and money he had saved. He put one bed against each wall with the crib against the fourth wall. "I'll put shelves above the beds next week," he promised.

Sunday was an important day for the Rusyn and Slovak women of Swoyersville, as church was a social event. There they met other ladies, gossiped, and made plans for afternoon gatherings and such. Gatherings always included music with the old instruments brought from the old country. When the music started, dancing and singing songs of the old country followed.

At one of these impromptu dances in someone's front yard on a summer evening, Dorotha noticed a young man dancing a polka with the young women, and laughing and joking around. He was handsome with black wavy hair and a mustache. She found out from a friend that his name was Walter, but she was too bashful to approach him.

One of the neighbors who had many grapevines in his backyard, was offering his homemade wine for anyone to taste. Walter and Pete sampled the wine several times and then Walter, while dancing to the music, accidentally bumped into Dorotha. He excused himself and went on dancing.

The next morning as Dorotha and Elizabeth rode the penny wagon down Kossack St, she noticed Walter and Pete walking down the unpaved street looking like they had a hangover, with their heads down and walking slowly. When Walter glanced at the wagon Dorotha waved at him. He managed to smile and wave back, despite his throbbing head.

A week later, while riding the penny wagon she saw Walter walking with a limp, then stumble up to the penny wagon and jump on. He smiled when he saw her and sat next to her. "Hello," he said in Rusyn, his hand bandaged.

"Hello," she said. "What happened to your hand?"

"I had an accident at work," Walter told her. "Cut my hand and bruised my leg. I'll be better soon. I'm well enough to work."

"Be careful," she said. "Your wife doesn't want you hurt."

"I'm not married. How about you?'

"No, I'm not married," she said blushing.

"What's your name?" Walter asked.

"Dorotha. This is my sister Elizabeth."

"Hello Elizabeth, I'm Walter. You two look like sisters, both pretty," he flirted.

"Thank you," each girl said smiling.

"Where are you from?" Walter asked.

"Austro-Hungary," Dorotha answered. "We're Slovak.

"I can tell," Walter informed. "I'm Rusyn, but our village is in Austro-Hungary in the mountains near the Polish border."

"What village?" Dorotha asked.

"Osturna, up by the Tatra Mountains," he answered. "What about you girls?"

"Klemburk. It is near Presov," Dorotha pointed out. "We have a lot of Rusyn that live in our village. That's why I understand Rusyn."

"Your village is not far from Osturna, about 200 kilometers," Walter said. "We learned some Slovak in school."

"How long did you go to school?" Dorotha asked.

"Until I turned twelve."

"Same here," she said.

"Got to get off here," Walter realized. "Nice to meet you, Dorotha and Elizabeth."

The next day Walter took the wagon again and sat next to the sisters. Elizabeth told him that her boyfriend and she were going to the Fall Bazaar at St Mary's. "Why don't you and Dorotha come with us?" Elizabeth asked.

"Sounds like fun," Walter agreed. "I'd like that. Dorotha, would you like to?"

"Yes, let's go with them," Dorotha said knowing her and Elizabeth's plan worked.

When time came for the Bazaar, Dorotha wore her best dress and put curls in her hair. Marika and her boyfriend, Anthony, a widower she knew from the mill, came along with Elizabeth and her boyfriend, Vincent, as chaperones. With all the supervision Walter was afraid to hold Dorotha's hand, but they enjoyed each other anyway.

As the months passed, everyone assumed that they would be getting married because they spent a lot of time together. But they were still supervised by a chaperone on each date. Dates in 1901 were a walking event. You walked to church, work, the stores, or to a park. Their favorite dates were to a party, or to the ice cream parlor at the drug store on Main St, always with a chaperone behind them. Marika took her responsibility of watching out for her nieces seriously.

A letter came for Walter from Josef at Christmas time. He wrote that he was loading railroad cars at work and was hoping to get a job as a switchman. He was now married and expecting his first child. He wrote that Grigory was coming to America after the spring planting in April, and was planning to go to Chicago to look for work. Grigory would first visit Ilko and Andrew for a few days, before going to Swoyersville for a few days on his way to Chicago.

1902 began as a year of weddings. First Marika married her widower boyfriend at St Mary's with a reception at the church hall afterward, paid for by the groom's family. Walter and Dorotha danced to the band many times, with Walter kissing Dorotha for the first time as chaperones too were busy to notice. Marika and her husband rented a home in Forty Fort, just over the railroad tracks on Slocum St.

A month later, Elizabeth married her coal miner boyfriend in a ceremony at St Mary's. She couldn't afford to have a reception at the hall, so Gabriel had the reception at his home with friends playing instruments so guests could dance on the lawn. After a few minutes of music being played, most of the neighbors came over to join in, each bringing food with them. The party went on even after the bride and groom were gone.

Dorotha now shared her room with just two toddlers. She hoped that going to weddings would put ideas in Walter's head.

"My brother Grigory is coming by for a visit on his way to Chicago around the first of May," Walter told her after Elizabeth's wedding, as they sat on Gabriel's porch. "We will need to have a party when he comes by to celebrate his coming to America."

"Maybe we can celebrate something more," Dorotha suggested.

"Like what?" Walter wondered.

"Oh, I don't know," Dorotha hinted. "We had fun at the wedding receptions."

"That's an idea," Walter said smiling. "Do you know of anyone having a wedding then?"

"Oh, a lot of boys ask me out," Dorotha teased. "Maybe one of them will ask me to marry him."

Walter sat back for a minute with a concerned look on his face as they sat on the porch. "I would rather you marry me than one of those ugly guys."

"Are you asking me to marry you?" Dorotha asked with a smile.

"Yes, I guess," he admitted hesitantly, surprised at what he said. "Should we get married when my brother is here?"

"That would be nice," Dorotha giggled and put her arms around him, as she covered his face with kisses. Overheard by others, word spread fast and soon most of the neighborhood knew about another upcoming wedding.

That night Walter wrote one letter to home and another to New Jersey. Dorotha also wrote home. It would be a simple wedding with a reception at Gabriel's home.

Dorotha sewed a new dress and embroidered it with the help of her sisters. They made a veil for her and bought her new shoes.

Grigory was best man and Elizabeth was bridesmaid. Father Volansky performed the wedding mass as he had for Dorotha's sister and aunt. The reception went on for hours with Walter and Dorotha dancing and being toasted by everyone until the evening arrived with rain, ending the festivities, as the bride and groom left for a hotel on Wyoming Ave. It was the first time either had been in a hotel.

Grigory, who told Walter that he wrote his name as George Wascura at Ellis Island, left for Chicago the next day. Ilko and Andrew couldn't make it as both of their wives were due to have babies any day.

Walter and Dorotha rented half of a double block at 97 Kossack St. With both of them working they could afford the rent and buy furniture. They rented the second bedroom to Pete. It was just like Gabriel's place, 2 rooms downstairs, two upstairs, and an outhouse out back. A coal stove was in the kitchen with an ice box to keep things cold. Being no one was at home on the days the ice man came by, they let the next door neighbor let the ice man in, and gave her the money to pay him.

With both working they were better off than most coal miners who had a wife and children to support. With both growing up where their families had little cash, they now had the opportunity to save money and even considered a bank savings account. They heard how the bank would give you interest for the money you deposited. "We need to save for clothes for our children and not spend it at Stanley's," she would tell Walter. "Besides you and I need to be in the garden after work. When I get pregnant, we will no longer have my salary."

In addition to a garden in the back yard, they also put in a chicken coop. Dorotha knew that when she was pregnant she would have to quit working, so she spent as much time in the garden as possible to save money. There was talk of a strike by the union, so that became an additional reason to save money and tend to the garden. Over half of the miners were members of the union, as was Walter.

Northeastern Pennsylvania was the major anthracite coal region in the US. Anthracite coal burns cleaner than bituminous coal, and was thus preferred in residential use in stoves and furnaces, as well as in steam locomotives. In May 1902, the union was asking for a twenty present increase in wages and a minimum daily wage. The union wanted a nine hour day instead of ten, and also wanted a way of confirming the weighing of the coal by mine operators. In addition, they wanted a way of addressing grievances with mine operators.

The mine operators refused to negotiate with the union and refused to recognize the union as they never had a contract with the union. So on May 12, 1902 the union voted to strike. On June 2nd, the maintenance workers at the mines joined the strike.

The Macarthur mine told the miners they were welcome to work in spite of the strike at most mines, and some miners did continue to work. The mine hired guards to keep striking miners from keeping the non-strikers from going to work.

On June 8 President Teddy Roosevelt had his Commission of Labor compile a report about the mine strike. Meanwhile Walter and Pete kept working. The union said they would accept arbitration or mediation, but the mine operators refused. In August Walter and Pete stopped going to work, feeling the pressure from neighbors and friends to join the strike. The garden was ready to harvest, and they were getting plenty of eggs from the chickens.

In September the price of coal was increasing dramatically. Roosevelt met with the mine operators and the union on October 3. He offered to mediate the dispute. The union agreed, but the mine operators refused. Finally on October 11, the mine operators agreed to arbitration by a committee. The committee consisted of a military engineer, a mining engineer, a federal judge from eastern Pennsylvania, a veteran of the coal industry, a Catholic clergyman, a labor representative, and the President's Commissioner of Labor. Roosevelt appointed the members of the committee, and the strike ended on October 23. Walter and Pete were back to work.

The commission held three months of hearings. The following March the commission awarded the workers a ten percent wage increase, a nine hour workday, workers were allowed to elect their own check scale man, and a grievance commission was established comprising of three people selected by mine operators and three people selected by miners. The mine operators still refused to openly acknowledge the union.

There was dancing at various parties in the coal mining towns on their first payday after being back to work.

Chapter Six

Children

Father Volansky announced on Sunday in the spring of 1904, that a new Byzantine Catholic church was being built on Tripp St in Swoyersville. It would be wood frame with an onion shaped steeple like those in the Carpathian Mountains.

"That's wonderful about the new church," Dorotha said that evening as they sat around talking after dinner with Marika and Elizabeth. "It will be so close. Just about a mile away."

"We'll be gone by then," Marika said. "The mill is promoting Anthony from supervisor to assistant department manager at their Cleveland Mill. We have to move at the end of the month. He goes next week to find us a place."

"Oh, I'll miss you so," Dorotha said.

"I think Vincent and I will be gone too," Elizabeth informed. "His brother wants him to come to New Jersey and help him run his business. He is offering more money than what Vincent earns at the mines."

"I hope it works out," Dorotha said.

"If it doesn't, we can always come back to the mines again," Elizabeth added.

"How have you been since your miscarriage last week?" Marika asked Dorotha.

"I'm better, thank you," Dorotha said.

"Don't worry, you'll be pregnant again many times, I'm sure," Elizabeth offered. She and Marika each had a child and both were pregnant again.

"I'm going to miss you both," Dorotha said as she looked at their toddlers playing on the floor. "Those two sure are playing nice with each other."

"Yes," Marika agreed. "But as cute as they are, I smell a stinky diaper."

Dorotha's sister and aunt had moved away by late summer, when St Nichols opened for its first service. Services were held in Old Church Slavonic. People in the area would call it the "Russian" Church, because many of the Rusyn were from the Carpathian Mountains in Ukraine, which was part of the Czarist Russian Empire in 1904.

Over the next two years, Dorotha went to the church as many times as she could each week to pray for a healthy baby. Her first pregnancy ended in a miscarriage. After a second miscarriage she would sometimes cry at night and Walter would console her. Whenever they visited friends, she would play with their babies, only to feel depressed afterwards. She would busy herself in the garden after work to take her mind off of it. She would write home to her parents each time she got pregnant, only to have to write again with the bad news. Finally she had a pregnancy that went full term in 1906. This time she decided not to write home until after the baby was born.

Just before Christmas, Dorotha woke Walter early one morning, telling him to go get Mrs. Rusinko. Mrs. Rusinko, a Polish Rusyn neighbor, sent her daughter to get other neighbor women. Soon five women crowded into the bedroom to calm Dorotha as she gave birth. The labor had not taken long.

"It's a boy," Mrs. Rusinko yelled to Walter who was in the next room. "What will you call him?" she asked.

"Walter Jr.," he answered.

"Come see," she yelled to Walter.

He went into the room and saw Dorotha smiling and holding a sleeping baby with black hair. He kissed Dorotha. "He is so tiny," Walter observed.

"He was just born," Mrs. Rusinko informed. "What did you expect? Now we are going to get the baby to nurse. So you go tell your friends that you have a son, while we help momma and baby."

Walter and Pete both left, and stood on Kossack St telling everyone passing by that Walter had a new son.

The baby had trouble nursing as Mrs. Rusinko had feared. The baby looked weak and was small for a newborn. "We will have to keep our eye on this one," Mrs. Rusinko told Dorotha and the other women. "He is not a strong baby, not yet."

Over the next several months, Walter Jr. was not putting on as much weight as the women had hoped. Twice they took him to the doctor's office. Medicine didn't seem to help either. At his baptism, the priest said an extra prayer for the baby to grow strong. After six months he started to put on enough weight to satisfy the women, although he did catch colds easily.

In the fall he caught another cold, so Dorotha put the basinet close to their bed so they could listen to his breathing at night. One night the baby stopped breathing as they slept, and they woke to find their baby dead. Walter ran screaming to the neighbors, so the women could come to comfort Dorotha. Pete went to get the priest. Another neighbor got some wood and started to make a small coffin, while one of the women made a lining for it. The next day neighbors walked with Walter, Dorotha and the priest to the end of Kossack St, then up the hill to Mountain St and the St Nickolas Cemetery to bury Walter Jr. The priest preached the grave-side prayers as the sun broke through the clouds.

In 1907 infant mortality was high as many diseases could overcome an infant. Many medicines were not developed yet. Still, when an infant died, there was deep grief felt by the parents. Dorotha cried for many days.

Dorotha went to church every day to pray for her lost son. She cried when alone in the house. The neighbors advised her to go back to work to busy herself. They told her she was still young and would have many more chances of having children. "I predict that you will have more children than you ever thought," Mrs. Rusinko consoled her. "You have talked to Father Volansky, and he has told you the same. He is keeping you in his prayers, as are all your neighbors. Bless you child."

In 1908 Walter got a letter from his youngest sister Kate announcing that Marya had married Peter Rusnak and that the entire town had come to the wedding. It was their parent's first daughter to get married. She wrote that their parents cried at the wedding mass at St Michaels, and that there was a long celebration with plenty of singing and dancing and toasting with wine.

Walter remembered Peter, a neighbor in Osturna several years younger than he. She wrote that Marya was 16 and Peter 20. Kate also wrote that she planned on getting her grammar school diploma. She would be the first in the family to do so. Kate was 11 now. Their sister, Annie, had just recently quit school. Kate wrote, "Dad hired Vasil Smolenak, Ian's son, to help with the farm. He is 18 and very nice. Peter's older brother Mark lives in Chicago and Peter and Marya are planning to come to America in a couple of months and stay with him. By the time you receive this letter they will be on the way.

Aksinya, who is now 21, plans to go with them. Mom and pop are a little upset because it will be just me and Annie left here. No one has returned as mom had hoped. Dad is going to be 57 soon. I told them not to worry, I will always be here to help them." The letter was dated two months earlier, which was about average time it took for mail to arrive.

Walter had often wondered about going back, but he would only go back if he bought land. He felt the hilly land was better suited for grazing. But you need more land for grazing then farming, and you needed to buy livestock, which meant you needed more money; more money than he had saved. He could stay here and buy a house with a big yard for a garden, as a lot of his friends had. Here, he had lots of friends who spoke his language, making it almost like being back in the old country.

Late one afternoon, two weeks after Walter had received the letter, he arrived home from work to be greeted by "Yuckshamash" as he opened the door. His sisters ran to him with hugs and kisses. "My, you two have grown so much," Walter commented. "It has been nine years. You two were seven and twelve years old when I saw you last. How long have you been here?"

"We got here just before Dorotha came home," Aksinya said. "We waited on the steps. This is a nice house you have here."

"This is my husband, Peter," Marya said.

"You were just a little boy the last time I saw you," Walter told Peter. "Let me get these work clothes off and wash my face."

When he got back from changing and washing, his sisters were helping Dorotha prepare supper for everyone, talking nonstop. Peter told Walter that they had spent a week with Ilko and Andrew and their families before coming here. "They still live close to each other," Peter told him.

"They always were together all the time, even as boys," Walter told Peter. "You never saw one without the other."

"They spell their last name Westura," Peter said.

"Yes, but George, Josef, and I just changed the V to a W," Walter said.

"I just spelled my name as is, Rusnak," Peter said. "Marya dropped the a at the end of her name to be Mary, and Aksinya wrote her name as Suzie Wascura."

"Suzie, I like that," Walter said. "Sounds American."

After supper, Suzie told Walter and Dorotha of instructions their mother had for them. "Mom says, that the next time Dorotha gets pregnant, she is to stop working immediately, and stop working in the garden," Suzie instructed. "Just have her take it easy. Eat plenty of cabbage, potatoes, eggs, and chicken, she says. She needs more meat on her bones to carry a baby anyway."

106

"I promise," Walter agreed.

"Then I guess I should be giving notice at the store," Dorotha informed.

"Why, are you pregnant?" Walter asked, eyes wide.

"I think so," Dorotha said. Walter gave her a hug, followed by everyone else.

"That calls for a toast and a prayer," Walter suggested. He found a bottle of wine in the cabinet that he had been saving for a special occasion.

Their prayers were answered in March, 1909 when Dorotha woke Walter early one morning before the sun was up. "Go get Mrs. Rusinko and tell her I need her."

"Is it time?" Walter asked.

"Yes, don't worry, just go get her," Dorotha told him.

Mrs. Rusinko and three other women stayed with Dorotha as her labor progressed. Walter told Pete that he would not be going to work that day. Walter paced downstairs until one of the women told him to go outside and feed the chickens, as it was going to be a while. Walter had a phone number of a doctor, just in case, and planned to run to Stanley's, where they had just gotten a phone. Stanley said he could use it if he had an emergency. Walter never had used one before. In the better neighborhoods like in parts of Forty Fort, families could afford for a doctor to come by in his horse and buggy, when the time was close. In Swoyersville someone would be sent for a doctor only in cases of emergency. A neighborhood collection would be taken to help pay for the doctor. Sometimes the doctor would go home with a pocket full of change and a chicken or pig in the back of his buggy as payment.

Early in the afternoon they called him inside. "It's a girl," he was told. "Dorothy said her name will be Anna."

"Yes, after both of our mothers," Walter informed.

"She is a healthy baby," Mrs. Rusinko said excitedly.

"I can hear her," Walter listened. "She has strong lungs."

"In a minute we will have her nurse," Mrs. Rusinko said. "That should quiet her."

"Thank God," he said as he walked in the room to kiss Dorotha, tears running down his face.

When Pete came home from work, the ladies told him to take Walter to the beer garden to celebrate, and let Dorotha and the baby sleep. "You boys be back in an hour," Mrs. Rusinko ordered.

That evening Dorotha and Walter talked as she breast fed the baby. "I'm going to teach her all the few English words I know, which is not many," Dorotha spoke softly. "I want all my children to get a grammar school diploma like your sister Kate is getting, and maybe even some high school. None of this only going to school until you turn 12."

"I agree," Walter said. "Everyone around here speaks a Slavic language, but the schools only teach in English, so Anna will probably be teaching us English. The good thing about this country, is there are public schools in every town and all the children go. There were some villages back home that had no one to teach the children."

The next day they wrote short letters home and to relatives around the US, announcing the healthy dark brown haired, brown eyed baby. Over the next months they got letters in return of more babies and marriages in their families. Suzie wrote that she married Peter's brother Mark Rusnak in Chicago. Mark worked for the railroad and got George and Peter a job on the railroad, she wrote. Ilko and Andrew's wives had more babies. Kate wrote from Osturna that Annie was wanting to come to America someday, but Kate was still promising their mother that she would stay with them.

Baby Anna became known as just Ann as her parents thought it sounded more American without the last a. Ann got a little brother named Jacob in July 1912. Walter bought cigars and went to Stanley's to buy everyone a beer. Then he went to church to light a candle for this son and pray that he would survive the Pennsylvania cold winters.

In 1912 in Pennsylvania, if a doctor was present at the birth he would fill out a birth certificate and send one copy to the county office for filing, and one copy to the parents. As often was the case, a doctor was not present at a birth, so the family would have the baby baptized at church by the priest or minister. The priest or minister would fill out a baptism certificate and would fill out a form to be sent to the local county office in most cases.

Jacob was born just in time for his Aunt Annie's visit. She had written that she was coming to America with her best friend and her friend's new husband. She wrote that Marya had offered to let her stay with them. Since Annie's friend and her husband were planning to go to Chicago, Annie would have companions for her journey. Being only 16, Mikel was concerned about her traveling at such a young age, but she pointed out that Marya was 16 when she went, and Annie was going with two older friends to the same US city.

"But Marya was married and went with an older sister," Mikel pointed out. But Annie had always been stubborn and he finally gave in. Mikel made her promise to visit Ilko, Andrew, and Walter on the way and write back about how they were doing.

"I had to borrow some money from mom and dad," Annie told Walter after she arrived. "I have to get a job quickly when I get to Marya's, so I can pay them back quickly. Dad didn't want me to go alone, so I had to come when my friend's here were coming. I hadn't earned enough yet, so I had to borrow."

"I know you will pay them back," Walter said. "You have grown to a young lady. You were three years old when I left. Kate was just two. Now you are full-grown. Time flies like a fast bird. Will Kate be coming next?"

"I doubt it," Annie said as she held Jacob. "She follows Vasil, dad's hired hand, all over the place. They are always working side by side. She gets sad when he goes home at the end of the day. She won't be coming unless Vasil does and she follows. But Vasil is a good farmer and I don't think he would be happy unless he was working outside. He has no money to buy a farm in America. He will stay there, and with Kate a few feet away from him. You have such beautiful children, Walter and Dorotha."

In 1914, with Dorotha pregnant again, Walter figured he would probably never be going back to Osturna, so he might as well become a US citizen. The miner's union encouraged all miners not born in the US to become citizens. The more miners that were voters the better for the union. In November 1911 he had applied for citizenship. He had studied for his test. On July 2, 1914 he and Dorotha rode the train with their two children to the Federal Courthouse in Scranton, where he would become a citizen. A few other miners were also with them to become citizens.

On the train back to Wilkes-Barre, a Welsh miner friend of Walter's, read an article in the newspaper to them about a war starting in Europe. Days earlier he had received a letter from Kate telling them of her wedding early in the year to Vasil

Smolenak. "Annie sure was right about those two," Walter told Dorotha. "I wonder if a war will involve that area. I hope the government won't make Vasil go in the Army."

When their baby Mary was born in October 1914, Walter and Dorotha had to go to St Mary's Church in Kingston for the baptism, because St Nicholas had a fire and was being rebuilt with brick. A friend had bought a model T Ford and offered to drive them to St Mary's. It was their first ride in an automobile. "It is appropriate that Mary is being baptized at St Mary's," Dorotha said as they rode down the street, waving at everyone in excitement.

It was a year of new technology for them. The previous week the landlord had electricity put to the house. Each room got an electric light in the center of the ceiling with a pull chain, and each room got an outlet. They had nothing to plug into outlets, so Walter bought two new lamps.

When they were at the store buying the lamps, they saw a used, hand-crank, Victrola phonograph with a cone shaped speaker. Ann and Jake, as they now called him, were excited with the phonograph. The children would dance or sing to some of the music on the two discs that came with it.

"What will they think of next," Walter told Dorotha, referring to the phonograph. "I saw an airplane flying over Swoyersville yesterday on my way home."

"Is that what that noise was?" Dorotha exclaimed. "Next time I hear a noise like that, I will look up."

In November, the day after Mary's baptism, Walter voted in an election for the first time. Dirty miners lined up at the polling place to vote, then headed to Stanley's where they knew politicians would be buying them some beers, and having some food on a table for them. The miners would often stuff some sausage and cheese in their pockets to take home.

Chapter Seven

World War

After Kate's wedding Mikel and Anna moved into the children's room downstairs. Mikel had gotten Anna a new bed and dresser for the room. Kate and Vasil moved into the upstairs bedroom, with a new mattress was made for the bed. Kate was 17 and Vasil 24, the age when most young people got married in Osturna, but recently, most either got married in America, or got married in Osturna and then moved to America like Mary and Peter. To marry and stay in town seemed to be the exception. So many people had moved from Osturna in the last twenty years that the population was now just over 1,400, over 500 people less.

The wedding was a typical Rusyn joyous celebration that lasted most of the day. The groom's family donned their finest colorfully embroidered shirts, vests, and skirts, and along with a fiddler, a flutist, and accordion player formed a procession to walk down the road to the bride's home. The musicians serenaded the procession from the rear. At the bride's home, the bride's family, also in their finest clothes, came out at the sound of the music. The music stopped as the Smolenak groom symbolically asked the Vascura parents for their blessing to marry their daughter. This was a formality, as it had already been asked weeks before. As Mikel and Anna gave their blessing, the bride came out of the house, and the procession continued on to the church with the musicians following both families.

After the wedding mass, the musicians played outside the church as the bride and groom came out, with the families following, singing and cheering. Everyone then walked to the tavern, followed by the musicians. Extra tables were set up outside the tavern to accommodate the number of people. When everyone was there, Father Mudrak asked for quiet as he then blessed a cup of wine. He handed the cup to the bride and groom to share, symbolizing a life together. Then everyone was given a drink to toast the couple after which the banquet started. When the bride and groom were finished eating they danced. As they danced a line of men formed, each holding coins to drop in a hat in order to have a short dance with the bride. The celebration went on after the bride and groom left for their new home.

As his children gradually left for America, Mikel had less farm help, so he planted less crops, and used more land for grazing or orchards. Soon to be 63, Mikel had given more work and responsibility to Vasil. Around Osturna, there were few fences and everyone let the grazing animals, cows, horses, sheep, and goats graze anywhere, as long as they didn't graze on crops. It didn't matter whose land it was or whose animal it was grazing on your land. Villagers would just brand their animal or hang a bell and tag around its neck.

A few days before Christmas 1914, Kate gave birth to a girl. Finally Anna had a grandchild she could actually hold, not thousands of miles away. With harvest over, Vasil had cash in his pocket for presents for his wife and baby. There was talk of electricity coming down the road to Osturna, but he would worry about that expense when time came to hook up, which may still be months or even years away.

It was late in the chilly afternoon, as he and the dog were moving the cows in toward the barn, when he saw three Austro-Hungarian army men coming up to the house.

He had heard that Austro-Hungary was drafting all men between 18 and 35 into the army for the war. The previous day they had been in town making lists of the eligible young men. Last June, a Yugoslav had assassinated Archduke Ferdinand of Austria in Sarajevo, and in July, Austria declared war on Serbia and invaded. Austro-Hungary had an alliance with Germany, the Ottoman Empire and Bulgaria. Serbia had an alliance with France, Britain, Russia, and Italy. So, Germany invaded France creating the western front. Britain, in turn, declared war on Germany. Russia invaded Germany and Austro-Hungary, creating the eastern front. Now at the end of 1914, Austro-Hungary was creating a Slovak Regiment to increase its Austrian and Hungarian Armies.

The three Army soldiers, a lieutenant, a Sargent, and a corporal, had come with a document for Vasil. Kate came to Vasil. "They have a draft notice for you," she yelled excitedly. "Tell them you have a child. They can't take you."

"I'll talk to them," Vasil worried. "Maybe if I limp, that will help."

At the house, Anna was giving the three soldiers a drink of apple cider she had made. "Why should Rusyn and Slovaks be fighting for the Austrians and Hungarians against the Russians and Ukrainians and other Rusyn in the Russian army?" Mikel asked the lieutenant.

"We are forming a Slovak Regiment to fight in the mountains to protect your villages from the Russian Army," the lieutenant explained to Mikel as Vasil walked in. Mikel handed Vasil the draft notice he had been reading.

"The lieutenant brought this," Mikel said as he handed it to Vasil.

"You are being drafted along with other young men from your village," the lieutenant said. "We are taking those eighteen to twenty-nine now. If we need more we will be back for those over thirty. But I think victory will come soon, so that will not be necessary. We will be back tomorrow to march you draftees to Propad to start training."

"What if I don't want to go?" Vasil asked.

"Then we have to arrest you and you have to go to jail," he answered with a smirk. "The war will be over by the end of the summer. With the help of the Slovaks and Rusyn, the Hungarians will crush the Russians and Serbs."

"You make it sound so simple," Vasil observed.

"What if someone has an injury and can't march?" Kate asked.

"The draftees will each be checked by the Army doctor in Propad," the lieutenant responded. "See you in the morning."

In the morning, almost a hundred draftees came walking down the road, led by the lieutenant and the Sargent on horses with the corporal bringing up the rear, also on a horse. The Sargent came to the door of the Vascura house.

"Vasil Smolenak," the Sargent said as he opened the door without knocking. "It is time. Let us go."

Vasil kissed Kate and his baby daughter. "I'll be home in a few months," Vasil said, as Kate and Anna cried. He then hugged her parents. Vasil's parents had come over from their house to say goodbye. He then left with the impatient Sargent and joined the other draftees.

Anna sat and cried. "Everyone leaves us," she complained.

Kate put her arm around her mother. "I haven't mom, I'm still here," Kate consoled her. Later that day, a letter came from Marya and that cheered her up as Kate read it to her.

At Propad the next morning, the draftees were given very quick physicals, plain wool uniforms, and old rifles. They were at the gun range by late afternoon. Tents were their new homes.

After four weeks of training, the new Slovak Regiment was transported in train boxcars, while the officers road in the passenger cars. The train headed to the mountains of the Polish area of Czarist Russia. The officers in the Regiment were all Hungarians, and bullied the draftees who were all Slovaks and Rusyn. The draftees were not enthusiastic about fighting against their fellow Slavs - the Russians, and Serbs.

In February the regiment joined an Austrian unit and a German unit north of the Masuria Lakes. They attacked the Russian Army in the middle of a heavy snowstorm. In the white snow the soldiers made easy targets in their dark uniforms, causing heavy casualties on both sides. Blood stained the snow red. Because of the mountains, resupplying the army was difficult, making food sparse. This made the soldiers weak against illness and frostbite. After Austrian and German advances for two weeks, the Russians were finally able to halt them and push them back.

Vasil, not wanting to kill anyone, would aim just a bit high, and hope he missed. When someone was wounded, he would stop and help the medics pull them back away from the line of fire, then help the medics wrap bandages on them. Helmets were not issued to anyone in his regiment, so injuries to the head were high. The Germans were a better equipped army with helmets and more motorized trucks. Vasil's regiment just had wool Cossack hats. Vasil was shocked at the numbers of dead and wounded on both sides. It seemed to him that the winner of a battle was the army with the most soldiers still standing. The number of prisoners was a problem. Troops would have to march them to a nearby town which resulted in many escaping in the process.

When they camped at the edge of a forest just before Easter, Greek Catholic Rusyn priests sat in the woods and heard individual confessions. Infantry men stood in line in the cool spring air to confess their sins, kneeling on the forest floor. At Easter Sunday service in an open field, the Rusyn troops sang the Lord's Resurrection hymn in Old Slavonic. Nearby Rusyn-Ukrainian Russian prisoners in a barbed-wire corral joined in the singing of the hymns.

His regiment was next moved to southeast of Krakow in the Garlice area. The Austro-Hungarians and Germans moved in more heavy artillery and attacked the Russians in May. The noise of the artillery was deafening, causing Vasil to tear off a couple of pieces of cloth and stuff it in his ears. Recieving heavy losses from being bombarded by the artillery, the Russians had to retreat from the area. This enabled the Germans and Austrians to take Warsaw by August.

After some time in Warsaw, Vasil's regiment was sent to the Carpathian Mountains in the Ukraine area. Vasil was happy to be alive, but did not see the war ending any time soon as he had been told. Food was an irregular event. Some days you would be starving, some days you had plenty. Wounded would be sent back to the front before they were healed. He continued to help the medics and aim over enemy soldiers whenever he was sent to the front.

Ambulance trucks with a Red Cross on the side drove around after a battle so wounded could be rushed to tents set up as aid stations. The badly wounded were left on the field to die, while those that could be saved were put on trucks. When they ran out of stretchers, wounded would be carried by their arms and legs to the ambulance.

Once when a battle was still raging, Vasil put a man with a leg wound over his shoulder, and walked with him to the aid station. The man, his head at Vasil's back, thanked him just before an artillery explosion went off. Vasil increased his pace. When he reached the aid station and placed the soldier down, he realized the man was dead with a piece of shrapnel in his head. The shrapnel would have gone into Vasil's back, if the man's head were not in the way.

After all of the wounded had been taken to the aid station, Vasil would be assigned to burial detail. Soldiers would take dead bodies to horse-drawn wagons and toss the bodies into it. Meanwhile, other soldiers would be digging a large pit about four feet deep. Into the pit, bodies would be tossed, after boots, ammo, helmets, or items from pockets were removed. All this equipment was tossed into another wagon for reuse. When the pit was full of bodies, laid shoulder to shoulder, lime was tossed over the bodies, covering the different colored uniforms of the Russian, German, Austrian, and Hungarian, turning them all white and ghostly. Now they were all of the same army of the dead. A priest from a nearby village would say prayers as dirt was shoveled on top of the bodies. One wood cross was placed at the center of the pit.

Whenever there was a charge at the enemy Vasil would be sure to run slow, and stop to help the wounded. Changes of clothes happened seldom and he and everyone else smelled like rotting fruit. Everyone's smelly beard grew, so they shared combs and scissors to keep their beards and hair trimmed.

The boots they had been issued wore out quickly. They would have to stand in line to have them resoled. The soldiers would share needle and thread to put patches on clothes. If a soldier had a torn coat, they would just take one off of a dead soldier of similar size.

Between battles, the soldiers of the regiment talked frequently about the Czechoslovak Legion that was being formed in late 1915. Slovaks and Czechs were leaving the Austro-Hungarian Army to fight for the Legion on the side of the Allies (the Russians, French, and British) against the

Austrians, Hungarians, and Germans. The men did not discuss this in front of the Hungarian officers. Leaders of the Czechoslovak Legion went to the Allies to present the idea that the Austro-Hungarian Empire should be dismembered and that Czechoslovakia should be an independent state. The Legion then formed the Czechoslovak National Council. Their goal was to win the Allies support for their Legion. If they could get the Allies to support them with money and weapons for a Legion Army, then they could fight on the side of the Allies. Since most Rusyn lived in the mountains of the Ukraine area, they were fighting in the Russian army against the Rusyn in the Slovak regiment of the Hungarian Army. Vasil knew he had to join the Legion whenever he got the chance.

The January 1916, winter weather in the Carpathian Mountains of Ukraine was harsh. The snow covered their tents until they collapsed. Frostbite was common. Supplies were slow and not enough. In March plans were being made secretly by the soldiers of the regiment to leave at night, and head to a nearby Russian Army unit that would be expecting them. The Hungarian officers couldn't find out or they would be shot for desertion. When the night came, those on guard duty went first. Then, under the dark of the moonless night, soldiers left their tents, taking their weapons and backpacks with them. About a fourth of the regiment left that night. More would come later. At daybreak, they met at their preplanned gathering place and stripped off their army insignia, leaving only their rank. The Russian army had armbands for them that said 'Legion' in Cyrillic. Over time the Russian Army would release some Slovak, Czech, and Rusyn POWs to join the Legion. Officers of the new Legion were Czechs, Slovaks, and Rusyn promoted from corporals and sergeants. Only the general was Russian, as previously arranged.

In June, the Legion had its first test as a fighting unit for the Russians. The Legion was used mainly to act as support, moving supplies, helping at the first aid station, hauling ammo to the front lines, cooking, and digging latrines. Few were on the front lines at first. Vasil volunteered to help with the stretchers, carrying wounded to the first aid station. In the battles to take back the cities of Lviv and Kovel, the Russians dug entrenchments all along the front line. The Russians crept to within 100 yards of the Austrian line as a massive artillery barrage bombarded the Austrians. The Russian advance was successful. The Austro-Hungarian Army suffered a majority of the casualties. Afterward the Austro-Hungarian Army had to rely on the support of the German Army. By September the Russians had met their goal and were planning their next strategy.

By the end of the year, Vasil had seen so many dead and wounded in two years. He had dug so many graves, helped bandage so many wounded, and carried so many stretchers, that he longed for the peace of home and the farm. Vasil had a good friend that he would sit and talk with; a Slovak from Klemburk named Vaskos Djurkan. One day as Vaskos was trimming Vasil's hair, Vasil told him, "I was thinking how lucky my wife's older brothers and sisters were not to be in Europe during this war."

"For now anyway," Vaskos pointed out. "How much longer are the Americans going to stay away?"

"True," Vasil agreed. "In the meantime, the Americans are making a lot of supplies being used in the war."

"Somebody is getting rich," Vaskos observed. "And it is not us."

"Wouldn't it be nice to not live under a monarchy that wanted their subjects to fight over land and borders to expand their Empires," Vasil wondered. "I hope when the war is over that the Czechoslovak Legion succeeds with their plans."

"Me, too," Vaskos said. "It would be nice not to be in a monarchy. I have two older sisters in America and their husbands vote."

Many a day, Vasil wanted to desert and start walking home. He wouldn't be the first. More and more troops were joining the Legion, making the Austro-Hungarian Army smaller. The Legion getting bigger helped the Russians as their Army was getting smaller due to political problems in Russia that were resulting in a Revolution. In February 1917 Tsar Nicholas of Russia abdicated the throne with the forming of a new provisional government. A Russian civil war continued, however, resulting in fewer Russian troops in the Carpathian Mountains of Ukraine.

#######

With German subs sinking US ships that were bringing weapons and supplies to the Allies, the US declared war on Germany in 1917. A draft was started in May for those men twenty-one to thirty.

With Ann eight years old and finishing second grade Walter started buying the Sunday newspaper, and Ann would read the paper to Walter and Dorotha with the help of a fifth grade neighbor. The kids liked the funnies the best. Walter was interested in the news of the war. Kate's husband was fighting in the war, as well as Dorotha's younger brother, Vaskos. Walter, while his spoken English was improving, did not know how to read many words, so it was newspaper reading by committee with the children.

In August the draft was expanded to the ages of eighteen to forty-five, and Walter had to register for the draft, being he was now a US citizen. The past October they had their fourth child, Michael, so Walter was told that he would not be drafted because he had four children, and his occupation, a coal miner, was considered important to the war cause. He had some friends who had not become citizens and were from Austro-Hungary. They were ineligible for the draft and were considered enemy aliens. Some considered becoming citizens. But the army would let them enlist whether citizens yet or not.

That year, Walter and Dorotha bought an old house at 225 Kossack St. It was a one story house with wood lap siding and a stone foundation. The basement was only half below ground, four feet being below ground, and four feet above. You went up six steps to the front porch. In the basement was the kitchen and dining room and a cellar room that contained a coal furnace. Steam radiators heated the main floor. The coal stove heated the chilly basement and included an oven as well as cook top. Next to the coal stove was a small hot water tank with pipes that went next to the coal firebox of the stove. Now as long as she was burning coal in the stove, Dorotha had hot water at the house's only sink that was in the kitchen. Next to the coal furnace was another small water heater for the steam heat system that led to the three radiators on the main floor. In the hot summer you unfortunately had to start a coal fire in the stove in order to cook.

The main floor had four rooms; a living room, a small bedroom, and two larger bedrooms. The house was only 18ft wide by 36ft long. The kitchen had a hand-pump for pumping water from the well. The outhouse was 30ft from the back door. As at most houses, boots were kept by the back door in case of snow on the ground when you needed to go to the outhouse. The house sat to one side of the 60ft wide lot with an apple tree in the side yard.

The house had electricity with one overhead light and one outlet in each room, but no telephone was in the house. They planned to get one someday when they felt they could afford the expense. The house had plumbing because the town had installed in a water system and run lines down the street.

But using the water was a monthly expense, so she used the well pump most of the time, as did many of her neighbors. The one luxury she allowed herself was the hot water heater whenever the coal fire was burning. With no bathroom in the house, baths were still in the big round tub, which was stored in one corner of the kitchen with a curtain around it for privacy.

Kossack St was still not paved, so dirt on shoes was always a problem as well as dirt from the garden. The youngest children often didn't have shoes to wear, so a carpet was at the door where they had to wipe their feet. Dorotha made Walter strip down to his underwear at the back door when he got home from the mine, and go to the tub.

What Walter and Dorotha liked most about the house was the long backyard. The lot was 120ft long with the house close to the front of the lot. In early spring they started planting in the entire back yard. The baby slept in a basket as the children helped drop seeds in the soil, even two year old Mary.

Walter would look for scraps of wood on his way home from work each day. By fall he had enough scraps to make a chicken coop and the start of a shed and fenced pen for pigs. The large garden would allow them to sell vegetables to neighbors, as well as can vegetables to store in the basement furnace room. Eventually, he also made a six foot wide swing with a back like a couch. It had a roof over it, supported by railroad ties and hung with chains. Dorotha could sit on it to breast feed babies between working in the garden.

#######

The Czechoslovak Legion had grown to three regiments in the Carpathian Mountains. In July 1917, the Legion attacked the entrenched Austro-Hungarian Army near Zborov, after an initial artillery bombardment. After advancing into enemy territory, they broke through the entire Austrian trench line, capturing many guns and artillery that they badly needed. Vasil was hoping this victory would bring an end to the war. Like so many in the Legion, he longed for home, but they knew if they went home, they might be shot for desertion by the Hungarians who they had deserted from the previous year.

In October of 1917, the socialist Bolsheviks controlled Russia, as their civil war continued, resulting in Russia being less involved in the eastern front. In March 1918, the Russians signed a peace treaty with Germany, leaving the Legion to have to defend the city of Bakhmach in the Ukraine. Eventually, the Legion was victorious and negotiated a truce. Afterwards, some of the Legion headed east, while Vasil and the others headed west into the Slovak area. As they marched west, that spring of 1918, he and Vaskos talked about home.

"It is planting time," Vasil said to Vaskos.

"Yes and we are not far from my home," Vaskos pointed out. "We should be there helping."

"We should stop by your village for a rest," Vasil suggested.

"I don't think the officers want to go south from here," Vaskos wondered as the regiment in line through the forest.

"I didn't mean everybody, just us," Vasil said as he put his arm on Vaskos shoulder, pushing him out of line to behind a tree. He whispered, "If we stop by some bushes to relieve ourselves, bend over and wait for all to pass, then we won't be noticed when we go in a different direction."

Vaskos eyes widened, "I like that idea. Excuse me, I have to go behind that bush."

"I think I will use that one," Vasil said as he went about ten feet away.

In twenty minutes all soldiers, wagons, horse drawn artillery, and a few trucks had passed. Vasil whispered to Vaskos, "Do you know where we are?"

"Yes, we are just north of Presov," Vaskos whispered back. "My village is 20 kilos west of Presov. I know how we can get there and avoid the roads and be there by night fall."

"Let's give them a few more minutes to get further away," Vasil suggested.

They hiked through farm fields, taking off their rank and insignias as they walked. They kept an eye out for any Hungarian Army. On the way to the village of Klemburk, they saw the effects of war, with land scarred with shell holes, trenches, and mass graves. When they passed near a village, some houses had been burned and some damaged. Even the churches did not escape the damage of artillery.

"I hope my village is not damaged," Vaskos worried.

As the evening started to darken to night, Vaskos yelled excitedly, "There it is, my home. It is fine, no damage."

He started to run. He didn't stop until he got to his parent's front door. He opened it as he said, "What's for supper?"

After his mother, Ania, screamed and hugged him until he thought she would never let go, Vaskos turned and introduced Vasil to his parents.

"Nice to meet you, Mr. and Mrs. Djurkan," Vasil smiled.

"Come sit. I make food for you two," Ania said. "You boys are skin and bones. You must be starving."

Vasil rested the next day, eating and sleeping all day as Vaskos made plans with Juraj about what they would be planting. Mrs. Djurkan washed Vasil's clothes. The following day Vaskos and Juraj took Vasil in a wagon to a town west of Klemburk where Vasil could catch a train to Propad. They insisted on buying him the ticket. They gave him a bag with bread and sausage and cheese to eat on the way.

"Give your wife and baby a hug for me," Vaskos instructed Vasil.

"I will," Vasil said hugging his friend. The next day he walked down the road leading to Osturna. The closer he got the faster he walked.

The winds from the mountains brought the pleasing smell of the trees and flowers, refreshing the air like a promise of better life ahead.

As the house got closer he started to run. Villagers in the fields saw him running and someone recognized him and yelled his name. Kate heard the villager yelling "Vasil" and turned to see him running down the road. She saw a man much thinner than Vasil, with a beard and longer hair, but the closer he got, the more she recognized his smile and eyes. He tossed down his backpack and rifle as he ran across the field to her. They were both crying by the time she knocked him over in embrace.

Soon Mikel was embracing him as Anna came to him with a toddler in her arms. "This is your baby girl Pajza," Kate told Vasil.

"She is not a baby anymore," Vasil observed as he reached for Pajza.

"No, she is not," Kate said. "She is over 3 years old. It has been that long." Tears still flowed down her cheeks. Pajza held up 3 fingers to Vasil.

"That's right," he said and kissed his daughter.

Later after a meal with Vasil's parents joining in, Vasil said, "We can't let anyone know I'm here. I just left and didn't tell anyone. If somebody comes looking for me, I will hide."

"Everyone in town knows you are here, they saw you running down the street," Mikel said. "The Legion is volunteer, and they aren't looking for people who go home for planting season. As for the Hungarians, their country is falling apart. The war is coming to an end in the east. In the west it was a stalemate until the Americans came over and started to beat up the Germans. Kate has been reading the newspaper to us each week. The new country of Czechoslovakia is being created, and the Allies have recognized the National council as the future government."

"That will be so good," Vasil said. "It is too bad so many have died."

"What about the other draftees in town that have not come home yet?" Mikel asked.

"Many will not be coming home," he answered, then began to tell them the names that he knew would never be coming home. Those that had come home before Vasil were wounded too badly to continue fighting. Kate was overjoyed that Vasil had made it home uninjured.

After a good night's sleep, Vasil was ready to help with the planting. Mikel walked slower now, but at 67 he looked more like 50. Anna and Kate promised to put weight back on

Vasil with their good cooking. After a shave and hair trim by Mikel, little Pajza planted kisses on his now bare cheeks.

In early November, a man from the neighboring town came riding his horse down the road to help a friend with some repairs, and told everyone that the war was over that night. "It takes effect at 11 o'clock on the 11th day of the 11th month," he yelled. "Tonight."

That night at 11 o'clock the church bells rang and Mikel and some neighbors opened bottles of wine to celebrate. Musical instruments were brought out at various impromptu singing and dancing celebrations throughout the village. Not only were they celebrating the end of the war, but the end of a monarchy governing their area, and the creation of a new government.

With the war's end, four monarchy empires disappeared: German, Austro-Hungarian, Ottoman, and Russian. New nations were created. Austro-Hungary was divided into four countries, Austria, Hungary, Czechoslovakia, and Yugoslavia. Transylvania was shifted from Hungary to Romania. The Russian Empire, which had withdrawn from the war at the end of 1917 during their Revolution, had become the Soviet Union and lost its western land as new nations of Estonia, Finland, Latvia, Lithuania, and Poland were created. Ukraine, however, would remain part of the Soviet Union. The Ottoman Empire became Turkey and other countries.

Czechoslovakia became a parliamentary democracy with a house of deputies and a senate. Peace was back and the people of Osturna were no longer subjects of a monarchy. The town was now part of the province of Slovakia. Townspeople were now going to be part of an election process.

#######

Prior to 1920, the miners were worried about a possible prohibition coming. The miners all enjoyed a cool mug of five cent beer to clear their throats of coal dust after work on their way home. If prohibition passed they would have to clear their throats with tea, or coffee, or soda, or water. Most of the miners voted for state representatives that planned to vote against the amendment. The amendment outlawing alcoholic beverages had to pass 36 of the 48 states to become federal law. Walter and the other miners liked the power of the vote. Unfortunately they did not get their wish, as it passed and would become law in 1920.

"I don't know what to do," Stanley, the owner and bartender of Stanley's, said to those at his bar the week before prohibition would start. "I'm going to go broke serving tea, coffee, and soda." Going into business had been easy. The beer distributor paid for the license and kept his cellar filled with kegs. He could serve liquor and wine also. He just had to pay the distributor each week as to how much he used.

"Can't you make your own," one of his regulars at the bar asked.

"It says here in the newspaper," Stanley said pointing at the paper. "Sale, manufacture, and transport of alcoholic beverages will be illegal. Consumption is not illegal. So no one can arrest you for drinking."

"Can someone make their own in their home," another customer asked. "Some of us make our own wine."

"It says you can make your own in your own home," Stanley read. "But you must consume it in your own home and not sell it."

"So I can keep making my own apple cider and wine," the man said.

"Yes," Stanley agreed. "Just don't sell any."

"But I can still trade it for food at the grocery store, I hope," the man wondered. "I have done that in the past to pay what I owed."

"Hey Stanley," Walter said. "Don't you live upstairs?"

"Yes, you know we do," Stanley said.

"So, you can make beer, wine, and cider in your cellar," Walter explained.

"That takes time," Stanley pointed out.

"Better get started," Walter suggested.

"But if the inspectors walk in and see people drinking, I will be arrested," Stanley objected.

"Put it in medal containers and metal mugs so no one can see what we're drinking," Walter suggested.

"Call it wheat juice, grape juice, or apple juice," another man said.

Another customer suggested, "Change your sign to Stanley's Coffee Shop. Sell sandwiches, ice cream, soda, coffee, and tea. On the wall have a sign that has what you serve and prices. But don't put juice on the sign."

"Right, customers will know to order the juice quietly," Walter agreed.

"Sounds like an idea," Stanley contemplated the ideas. "Are you guys going to bail me out, if I get caught?"

"We will take up a collection," One man promised.

The next day Stanley got books on making cider, wine, and beer. Then he got the equipment he needed to homebrew and set it up in the cellar. He kept the door to the cellar padlocked and hidden behind boxes. It would take time before his first batch of beer would be ready. In the meantime his customers grumbled about having to clear their coal dust throats with soda or something else. The distributor now kept him supplied with small kegs of soda flavors. Stanley's wife made cookies, pies, and ice cream to sell to the miners to nibble on as they drank their sodas, until the first batch of homebrew was ready.

Chapter Eight

From Prosperity to

Economic Depression

Mikel and Anna enjoyed getting letters from America as they would usually be announcing another grandchild. But, Anna could only imagine the baby, as she had only held one grandchild in her arms, Kate's little girl. However, in 1920 Kate had a baby boy to Anna's delight. With two grandchildren in the house now, Anna was always ready to help Kate. They named the boy Mikolas after an uncle.

Kate and Vasil's daughter, Pajza, liked to help her grandma make pyrohies. Pajza liked to add surprises to the filling of each pyrohy. As she put the potato and cheese filling on the doe, she might drop in a piece of kielbasa, or a piece of apple, or some sauerkraut, or a grape, or whatever edible was available, before folding over the doe. Everyone called the pyrohies 'Pajza surprises'.

Just before Christmas that year, a letter came from Walter. After she opened it and read, Kate yelled, "number twenty." She continued, "In November Dorotha had a baby boy, Andrew, their fifth child. They had a good garden this year, which came in handy as there was a coal miner's strike for a few weeks."

Osturna had a good harvest that year also, and Vasil bought lumber to add a room to the house for the children. With the help of some neighbors, he and Mikel dug a foundation on the side of the house where the stairs going to the loft were. Then they gathered stones from around town, especially by the creek. A neighbor owed Vasil a favor, as Vasil had helped plant the neighbor's field when the man was sick. This was another Osturna example of trading labor for labor or goods. This neighbor knew how to lay a good stone foundation with mortar. When they finished, they let it settle for a week.

After Christmas Vasil and Mikel laid the floor, then framed the room with another neighbor. It would be cheaper to use framing and siding instead of squared logs like the rest of the house. The neighbor's son had apprenticed as a carpenter in another village, and they would hire him to help with the frame, siding, and roof. Electricity and telephone were coming down the street on poles, so Vasil had the crews run lines to their house. Vasil figured he could put outlets and wires in the house when he had the money.

But with Christmas here, it was time for festivities. Since the war, he looked forward to these family times, having missed them during the war. The church had built a large room for gatherings, dances, and weddings. Kate loved to dance and sing and Vasil was learning the flute.

The population in Osturna was 1,400 people in 1920, down from almost 2,000 twenty years earlier. People immigrating to America, or moving to jobs in cities in Europe, or young men dying in the war, were the causes of population decline.

With the new government of Czechoslovakia, Vasil and Mikel got to vote for a representative to the district council, a representative to the Slovak provincial council, a representative to the house of deputies, and others. This voting was new to them and they took the responsibility seriously. The villagers would get information on the parties and candidates, and post them on the church board. The villagers read these information sheets to determine who to vote for.

########

In America, Swoyersville's population was growing. In 1920 the town had almost 7,000 people. Twenty years earlier there were just over 2,000 people. More homes were being built every day.

At Walter's Union Hall, the union would post information on the candidates they felt were friendly to the unions. In 1920 the women had the right to vote for the first time. The union was encouraging members to get their wives to register to vote, figuring they would be pro-union and that would be better for the union. But some immigrant wives had not become citizens yet, so that had to happen first, before they could register to vote.

With increased technology, the process in the coal mines for separating slate and rocks from coal became less labor intensive, therefore reducing the need for "breaker boys". It was now law that children under 14 could not work, unless in a family business, such as a farm. Also, children now had to be in school through the eighth grade. This pleased Walter and Dorotha as they didn't want their children to leave school until they had their eighth grade grammar school diploma. They wanted to have them get some high school too, at least until they turned 15.

Schools became crowded with all the immigrant children born in the United States, now of school age. Between 1880 and 1920 more than 25 million foreigners arrived on American shores. During this period most of the immigrants were from Southern and Eastern Europe. In an immigrant small towns like Swoyersville and other towns along the Susquehanna River, homes were being built, resulting in more property taxes were being collected that paid for more schools.

Overcrowding was a bigger problem in big cities like New York and Chicago. Immigration during the World War was greatly reduced from 1914 to 1918, but increased again after the war. With the exception of the war, over 800,000 immigrants were arriving annually. Prior to 1920 immigration had never been systematically restricted by federal law. That changed with the 1921 Immigration Quota Act which imposed a limit on the number of immigrants allowed to enter the US. It established different quotas for immigrants from each country.

The law specified that no more than three per cent of the total number of immigrants from any specific country already living in the US in 1910, could migrate to America during any year. This reduced immigration in the coming year. The 1924 Immigration Act changed the percentage to two per cent, further reducing the number of immigrants.

The Eastern Europeans brought their religion, customs, and traditions with them. Six Eastern Orthodox and Greek Catholic churches were on the west side of the Wyoming Valley of Pennsylvania. These were mixed in among the Roman Catholic, Lutheran, Episcopal, and other Protestant churches in the small towns.

One tradition of the Rusyn was to name a child after a saint if the child was born on the saint's day. The only exception would be if you already had a child with that name. In March 1923, Dorotha gave birth to their sixth child on St Joseph's day. Therefore, the baby boy was named Joseph. If it had been a girl instead, her name would have been Josephine. As he grew he would always be called Joe. Dorotha considered it a blessing that she had a child born on a Saint's day, and Joe would always have a special place in her heart. As she fed the baby, she remembered the old neighbor telling her not to worry, that she would have many children.

Walter and Dorotha were 41 when Joe was born but that would not be her last pregnancy, as a couple years later she gave birth to a premature stillborn girl. The last pregnancy was her thirteenth. Four miscarriages, two stillborns, and Walter Jr's death, left them with six growing, healthy, children.

Over the years, the children grew strong and helped in the yard. The boys had to feed the chickens and pigs. The girls gathered the eggs each morning. When a pig was full-grown, the boys would put a rope around its neck and walk it several blocks to the butcher shop and leave it. The next day they would take their little wood wagon to the butcher shop, and pick up half of the butchered pig, cut and wrapped into sections. When they got home Dorotha would cut off a small part of each section and put it in the ice box. The boys hung the rest of the meat on hooks hanging from the ceiling of their small smoke shed that Walter had built in the back yard. A smoldering coal fire in the floor of the shed would be waiting for the meat.

The boys also had the job to cut off the chicken head whenever Dorotha was planning chicken for dinner. They would hang it by its feet for a few minutes to let the blood drain out its neck before taking it to their mother or sisters to gut the chicken to prepare for cooking. The family couldn't cook too many chickens because it was their source of eggs.

The neighborhood boys liked to go to Stanley's Café (former beer garden) and stand next to the open door to listen to baseball games on the radio. Their mothers didn't allow them inside. Technically it was now a café, but the mothers knew better. Wilkes-Barre got a radio station, WBAX, in 1922, and the next year Stanley got a radio for the bar/cafe. The boys listened to the 1929 World Series when their favorite Philadelphia Athletics beat the Chicago Cubs 4 games to 1.

To maintain his home brew (juice) business, Stanley gave the local policemen almost daily free meals and gifts at Christmas time. This added expense caused a doubling of the price of a nickel beer to ten cents. Customers didn't complain. They were just happy to have a secret place for a beer.

On Joe's seventh birthday in 1930, he got knew pants, shirt, and socks to wear to school. He was so excited because he usually wore hand-me-downs from his older brothers. The next day when he got home from first grade, he found his dad home early from work, and his mom looked like she had been crying. His dad poured a glass of beer from a jug that he had filled at Stanley's cellar on the way home from work.

"Where are your brother's Joe?" Walter asked.

"Outside playing catch with the Shucosky brothers," Joe answered.

"Would you tell them to come in, Joe?" Walter instructed.

When the boys came in a few minutes later, Walter explained, "Boys, the mine closed temporarily. There is less demand for coal right now because the mills' and factories' business is down. The mine has railroad cars full, but not sold

144

yet. So until the coal is sold, they don't need us to mine any right now."

"Do you want me to take my new clothes back to the store?" Joe asked sadly.

"No, no, you keep wearing them. They are paid for," Walter reassured him. "The union will give each member $5 each week from the union's strike fund until it is used up. Spring is here and we can start planting. We can plant the side yard too. Hopefully this won't last too long. Jacob and Mary are working so that will help. You three boys can help in the yard after school. There is a chance that when the mine calls us back, it may just be for a couple days per week, so this garden will be important this year."

Conversations in the house were always spoken in a combination of Rusyn, Slovak, and a little English. The children spoke English rapidly if they didn't want their parents to know what they were saying. The children learned English at school. It wasn't a disadvantage, as most of the school children in the town were going to school not knowing much English. The three younger boys had an advantage, as they had older siblings that taught them some English before starting school.

Every square inch of yard was planted during the next month. Walter did leave space for flowers in the front yard for Dorotha. She liked to put fresh cut flowers in the center of the table on birthdays.

Over the next few years, the coal mines would close a couple of times a year for a couple weeks each time. Occasionally they would cut to three or four days per week, instead of five or six. At 60 cents per ton for the workers, one had to be frugal when you had a wife and children. Many times the neighborhood children tried catching fish in the pond behind the Wascura house. But the fish were always too small. They had better luck catching frogs. The pond would often dry up in the middle of summer. In winter it would ice over to the children's delight, as they would slide along the ice on their shoes. No one could afford ice skates on Kossack St in the 1930s.

Walter and a neighbor made Dorotha a new loom. She would make something with yarn scraps or scraps of cloth from the clothing factory in Swoyersville. She would make things to sell to anyone who had money, or for the needs of her family.

Walter would take in people's shoes to repair, or resole, or re-heel to earn extra money. Like many families, they had to earn extra money any way they could during the depression in order to keep food on the table, clothes on the kids, and coal in the stove.

In letters from Osturna and Klemburk, Walter and Dorotha realized Eastern Europe was also effected by poor economic times. Vasil was not getting good prices for crops on the market. He and some neighbors cut some of the nearby forest to create some more pasture, so they could increase their number of cattle and sheep. Osturna and Klemburk's populations remained the same.

Swoyersville's population however increased 30 percent from 1920 to 1930 to over 9,000 residents. With high unemployment after 1929, immigration slowed dramatically. Some state's labor laws changed to keep children in school longer, since there were few jobs for them. Children had to be 15 to work, and couldn't quit school until 16, unless they had a job and their parents' approval.

By the 1933 election people wanted change. Walter had his children read him the Sunday paper. He couldn't afford it every day. They read that Franklin Roosevelt, as governor of New York, had started state projects to give people jobs constructing roads, buildings, bridges, or parks in New York. "That's what the whole country needs," Walter told his children. "I'm going to vote for him. Besides he wants to repeal prohibition. Smart man."

State, local, and federal governments missed the taxes on alcohol. With prohibition, governments had to spend more to enforce it. The increase in crime involving alcohol was expensive to attempt to halt. With no regulation or inspecting of the production of illegal alcoholic beverages, illness and death by alcohol poisoning became a problem. No tax income and higher enforcement expenses doomed prohibition.

After Roosevelt's election, the Work Projects Administration, Conservation Corps, Social Security

Administration, and other changes passed Congress to help unemployed and elderly. Even Kossack St got paved with some WPA money and a sewer was laid at the same time.

Difficult economic times caused people to have to move to different areas. During the 30's Walter and Dorotha saw their older children move away. Ann and her husband, Stan, moved to the Philadelphia area to be near his family when the company he worked for went out of business. Mary and her husband, Bill, moved to the Philadelphia area also, after he had been laid off from his job. His family had a small business that he could work at until he could find something that paid more.

Jake had been working at a locomotive parts factory in Wilkes-Barre when it was closed by the parent company, Bethlehem Steel. Fortunately, he was offered a job at their Bethlehem steel mill at less pay. Less pay was better than no pay, so he moved to Bethlehem. After starting his new job he met a girl that would become his wife.

Mike had traveled to New Jersey to visit his cousins after being laid off in Swoyersville. There he found a job in New York City and stayed there.

By 1937, Walter and Dorotha found themselves down to just two children at home, Andy and Joe. With constant layoffs and short weeks at the coal mines, it was good they had less people to feed and clothe. They were proud of their four oldest children as each had obtained an eighth grade completion certificate.

Despite hard times, the people of Swoyersville still liked to have a good time. The boys liked to go to the Saturday afternoon movie matinees. In the fall they liked to go to the high school football games with their dad. The high school had a tough time making a team since so many boys quit school to help support their family. The church bazaars and church dances were big events. Andy had earned spending money doing odd jobs and bought a guitar and learned to play it for friends when they got together. Kossack St had many youngsters as most homes had children. Boys liked to toss a ball around on the street. They would use an old sock stuffed with paper or rags to play stick ball, the sock being the baseball, and a stick being the bat. An old football was a valued item. The neighborhood could play for hours with a football. Sometimes a mom would sew old rags together stuffed with more rags to make a cloth football.

When Joe started the ninth grade, he signed up for the freshman football team. Although strong for a 14 year old with no fat, he was only 120 pounds. He was too light for the line or the backfield, so he went out for the end position. He knew he was fast and could catch a pass. But Swoyersville, as was typical in 1937 high school football, ran the ball 90 percent of the time. So Joe's time on the field was spent blocking and tackling boys bigger than himself.

In the tenth grade he was a little bigger, but got into the varsity game seldom. He wasn't upset because he knew he would be bigger the next year. That winter, Walter got sick with pneumonia and was out of work for three weeks. There was no sick pay. When he got back to work, the coal mine had gone to four days per week. A month later there was a two week layoff and Walter got sick again. After almost 40 years in the mines, his lungs were clogged with coal dust and unable to fight off colds, bronchitis, or pneumonia.

Mike would send money home occasionally, but the other three were married with children and couldn't help. In February 1939 Walter sat Andy and Joe down to talk to them.

"We are really in bad times for money," Walter told them with tears in his eyes. "The only money coming in is you two boys' Saturday job at the grocery store. It hurts us to have to tell you boys that you have to go to work full time. Andy, you have only four months until you graduate. You will be the first Wascura to have a high school diploma. We're so proud. I hope the store can give you more hours in June. Joe, we are so sorry to have to ask you to get a full time job. You turn 16 in a month and can quit school. Mike wrote that he can get you a job at the Delicatessen that he is working at. He wrote that you and he can share a room at the rooming house where he lives. In a year things will be better, and you can come back and finish high school. You have been doing so well in school. You are the smartest in this family in math. A B plus in Geometry this year is excellent."

They all sat in silence for a couple of minutes, Dorotha wiping her tears, and Walter wiping tears as he blew his nose and coughed. Joe sat in silence, his world turned upside down, words escaping him, fighting back tears. He had planned to play football and graduate. Now economic reality was making him grow up fast. His dad's coughs were a concern for him. He had a couple friends whose dads could not work in the mines anymore because of a cough. Of course, Joe knew that if he were working, he would have money for new clothes, which he needed.

Dorotha finally broke the silence, "Joe, with Andy working more after June, and you and Mike sending money, we can save money so you can go back to school and finish."

"Yes, I want both of you boys to graduate," Walter added between coughs. Andy was relieved he was so close to graduating, and felt sorry for his little brother who he knew was smart.

Walter went walking through the frozen garden after the talk with the boys, standing at the edge of the frozen pond, upset at the decision he had to make. It had been 40 years since he came to America with his big dreams. Although his home was nicer than the one he grew up in, and much nicer than the one Dorotha grew up in, it was not the big house he had dreamed of. Whenever he would get ahead monetarily, something would happen to eat up his savings; a strike, a new baby, a work stoppage, a sick child, the 1936 flood that flooded his kitchen, and now his ill health. He never built on to the house as he had planned. His sketches of house additions lay in a kitchen drawer, never realized.

"Walter, get in the house," Dorotha yelled to him interrupting his train of thought. "You shouldn't be out in this cold weather."

"Yes, dear," Walter responded. "I'm going to the store and get a bottle of brandy. I'll drink that with some of that good potato bread you made. That will help my cold. The brandy relaxes my lungs."

Joe had a feeling that his dad's cough would be a continuous problem. Three weeks later, the day after his sixteenth birthday, Joe walked into the high school office and told the office lady he would be taking a year off, and would be back the same time next year. She had him fill out a form. She had seen this happen many times in the past ten years, many of whom didn't come back.

The next week, Joe rode the bus to the train station in Wilkes-Barre where he bought a ticket for Brooklyn. It was his first trip on a train. He had the address of the deli and of Mike's rooming house.

Upon arriving in Brooklyn, Joe walked to the deli first as he was hungry. He saw Mike behind the counter, so Joe walked up and ordered a ham on rye. Mike didn't recognize him as he started making the order.

"How you doing Mike?" Joe asked Mike.

Mike looked up and noticed Joe standing with a piece of luggage, then realized it was Joe who he hadn't seen in over two years. "It's my brother," Mike yelled smiling.

"Is this the one that is going to work here?" Mike's boss asked with a heavy Polish accent.

"Yeah, that's him," Mike answered. "This is Joe, everyone."

"After you eat, Joe, I have a form for you to fill out," the boss said to Joe as he handed him a plate with the sandwich. "Do you have a social security card?"

"Yes," Joe answered. "How much do I owe you?"

"It's on the house," the boss said handing him a bottle. "Here, have a coke, too."

As Joe sat at a table eating, Mike joined him. "You look just like dad in their wedding picture. Same nose and wavy black hair. Same height." Mike was the tallest of the brothers; Jake the shortest. They all had big noses, but Joe and his dad had the largest, not just long, but wide too.

"The New York World Fair is going to be starting in May," Mike pointed out. "We've got to go to that. It's going to be amazing."

"Sounds great," Joe said excited about all of the things he could see on his day off in New York. "Dad and Mom made me promise to visit the Statue of Liberty. They told me about the ship going right past it when they each came over from the old country."

"I'm off this coming Sunday," Mike told him. "I'll make sure you are off also. We're only open one o'clock to seven on Sundays. Other days we're open ten to nine. I'll take you on Sunday. We can take the ferry from Battery Park."

When Mike got off, he and Joe walked to the rooming house. It was a four story building with one room apartments. On each floor were two bathrooms, one at each end of the hall. Mike had switched to a new room. The new room had two beds, two dressers, a closet, and a cabinet for pots and dishe,s with a two burner electric hot plate. In the hallway, next to each bathroom was a big sink for people to wash dishes or wash clothes. The rooms had no plumbing. Mike had a clothes line hung in the room to hang drying clothes on. Occasionally he dropped clothes off at a laundry. This rooming house didn't have meals with the furnished room. Mike got a free lunch at work each day he worked. He kept kept food in the cabinet for other meals.

"We'll go grocery shopping each week together and split the bill," Mike told Joe. "No ice box, so we have to do can goods and such that can keep.

"You have a nice radio," Joe noticed.

"I like to listen to the music and the comedy shows," Mike said.

154

"Do you get the newspaper?" Joe asked, noticing the papers laying on the floor next to Mike's bed.

"No, but customers bring them with them to the deli, then leave them on the tables. So I bring them home with me, instead of throwing them away, when cleaning up the deli at night."

"I like to read the paper. I'll do the same."

"There's a library near here. We can get you a library card. You get to check out a book for two weeks to read at home for free."

"I'll definitely visit there."

On Sunday they went to early mass, then took the bus to Battery Park. There they bought tickets for the ferry to the Statue of Liberty. It was Joe's first ride in a boat. As they stepped off the ferry Joe was in awe at the size of the statue. It was 305 feet from ground to the tip of the flame. It stood on a 154 feet high pedestal, the statue itself standing 151 feet. They walked the 178 steps to the top of the pedestal and exited out the door to a viewing platform just below the feet of the statue. As they stepped out, the wind almost knocked them over. They walked around the platform where they had a good view of New York, New Jersey, the large train terminal, Ellis Island, and ships going by. The steps to the crown were not open to the public due to needed repairs.

That night, Joe wrote to his parents telling them that the Statue of Liberty was big just as they had described. Walter and Dorotha's ability to read English handwriting was very limited, but he knew they would have Andy read it to them.

After the 1939 World Fair opened, Joe and Mike got themselves scheduled off in the middle of the week since the weekends would be very crowded at the fair. The day they went, they rode the subway to Flushing Meadows early in the morning.

At the RCA exhibit at the fair, they saw television sets that they didn't know even existed. One set was made with a transparent case so that the internal components could be seen. As part of the exhibit, visitors could see themselves on televisions as they walked by the cameras. Joe and Mike went back in line a second time, so they could see themselves again.

The Westinghouse exhibit featured a seven foot tall robot that talked and even smoked cigarettes. There was a globe planetarium located at the center of the fair. There were displays of new technologies, like color photography, nylon stockings, air conditioning, and fluorescent lamps. Joe and Mike liked the display of the automatic dishwasher. "We need one of those at work," Joe commented.

At the Chrysler exhibit they watched a 3D film of a Plymouth car being assembled. The theater was air conditioned. This was the first time they were in an air conditioned building. It was new technology in 1939. "Do you realize," Joe said to Mike. "Nobody in our family owns a car or has a driver's license."

"Right, but everybody lives near a bus route they can take to work or shopping," Mike said. "Also, nobody can afford the car or the gas."

At the GM exhibit, they saw a display of a new streamlined diesel-electric locomotive. At the IBM pavilion, electric typewriters and a machine called the electric calculator that used punched cards, were on display.

At the Amusement area, they rode the roller coaster, a first for both of them. They also went on the parachute jump. In the amusement area was a Jungle Land of rare birds, reptiles, and wild animals. There were orangutans, three performing elephants, camels, and plenty of monkeys.

At the end of the day just before closing, Mike asked Joe, "Do you have enough money left to ride the roller coaster again?"

"Yes," Joe said as he looked in his pocket. "And just enough money to get back home. But then I'll have nothing until pay day. I won't be able to send money home for a while."

"It's OK," Mike said. "The World Fair only happens once."

Each week the boys would split the rent and pay the landlord, and then they would go shopping and split the cost. They would take part of what was left and put it in an envelope addressed to Swoyersville for Mike to mail. It might be $1 or as much as $4.

One week Mike said he was out of stamps. "I'll just keep it my pocket until I get some stamps," Mike told Joe.

The next day after work, Joe heard Mike's voice coming from someone else's room as he walked to their room. The door was ajar and Joe looked in to see Mike playing poker. Next to Mike was the envelope ripped open that had the Swoyersville money in it.

When Joe confronted him later, Mike said, "I had a chance to double my money. I could have sent them more than $2 extra."

"Did you double your money?" Joe asked.

"No."

"How much did you lose?"

"I just have 35 cents left."

The next week Joe caught Mike playing craps with the money for home. After that, Joe said he would send any left over money he had to Swoyersville in his own envelope.

Chapter Nine

Another War

At the end of 1939, Mikel and Vasil were worried that war was in the near future and that it might involve their town again. The buildup of Germany's army was a concern. Mikel, despite being 87, was still helping with the farm. Vasil had bought the house next door when that family moved permanently to Propad. Anna had difficulty moving around, being 84, and spent most of her time knitting and sewing clothes.

Vasil and Kate's oldest son Mikolas, 19, lived in the upstairs room of Mikel and Anna's house. Their oldest daughter, Pajza, was married and lived 20 miles away. Their three younger children shared a bedroom in Kate and Vasil's home. All three generations had dinner each night at Kate's dinner table.

"I hope, if war starts, they don't start drafting young men," Mikel commented one evening. "I remember what you had to go through in the last war Vasil."

"Do you think the German army buildup will result in war?" Vasil asked.

"Yes, they want to take over all of Europe," Mikel answered.

"They annexed Austria last year," Mikolas added. "Just marched in and took over. This last spring they took over the western parts of Czechoslovakia as so called German protectorates."

"That left Slovakia as an independent state, but under German so called protection," Vasil pointed out. "But now they brought their troops in and a Slovak army, made up of the old Czechoslovakia Army, reports to German generals."

"Who are they protecting us from?" Mikolas asked. "It's the Germans we need to be protected from."

"Now the Germans are having our army help them fight Poland," Mikel pointed out. "The Polish weren't going to let the Germans just walk in and take over their country, so the Germans attacked."

"Only the Polish didn't have enough army or modern equipment," Vasil added. "They got demolished."

"Now we got the Germans north, west, and south of us," Mikel complained. "Good thing we are up in the mountains near forest, so we can hide the cattle and sheep from the armies when they come looking for meat, like they did in the last war. I hid them good last time."

"Why did Slovakia just sign a treaty with Germany?" Mikolas asked.

"Fear," Vasil answered. "With a few German troops in Slovakia, we were forced to follow German demands in fear of what Germany might do."

"I figure Germany attacked Poland to get ready to attack Russia next," Mikel predicted. "They want Russian oil. Also, if they attack the Soviet Union, that will keep the Soviets from protecting Romania. The Germans want Romania's oil too."

"Their mechanized army thirsts for oil to make fuel," Vasil added.

Mikel and Vasil would be right. But first Germany attacked France in May 1940. In June 1941, Germany turned their attention to the Soviet Union and invaded. Mikel and Vasil were nervous that Mikel and other young men of the village might be drafted. They all kept an eye out for officials, but none came. "It pays to be back here in the mountains, at the end of the road, out of sight of the main roads," Mikel commented in the summer of 1941.

"That wasn't the case at the end of 1914," Vasil reminded.

"Back then, they just kept following the road drafting young men until they ran out of road," Mikel said.

161

"This time if the Germans are in need, they will tell the Slovak Army to draft more," Vasil guessed. "At least the Germans don't know this village is at the foot of the mountain peaks. If they come around we'll hide Mikolas, or send him to the forest."

"Last time, the Hungarians saw you in the field," Mikel reminded.

"But this time nobody likes the Germans, they just fear them," Vasil said. "I've been talking to other neighbors, and we have a plan to tell any draft officials that all the young men are in Propad and Presov working in the factories. With the Germans making Slovakia send the Jews to Poland, they need workers at the factories."

"I know a Jewish tailor in Frankova," Mikel observed. "He is afraid they are going to send him and his family to Poland. He will lose everything. He owns his shop, inventory, home, and land. He'll lose it all. What do they want with him in Poland?"

"They put them in work camps, and they work for food and a bunk to sleep in, no money," Vasil informed them with what he had heard. "The man from Kacwin who bought the young bull from us, told me. If I were a Jew, I would change the spelling of my name to a Christian sounding name, and put crucifixes everywhere; on the front door, on a necklace, on the wall, and hide the Star of David and anything else that suggests

Jewish. Any Germans, or someone acting on behalf of Germans come around, they won't be the wiser."

"How long do we have to put up with the Germans?" Mikolas asked.

"They are fighting two wars, like the last time," Vasil pointed out. "Fighting Russians on the east, and an air war with Britain on the west. They will eventually get squeezed like the last time. If the Americans ever join the war, they will be finished eventually like last time."

It wasn't too long for the Americans to join. Before 1941 was over, the Japanese attacked Pearl Harbor, and the US declared war on Japan and Germany.

#######

Late Sunday afternoon on December 7, Joe was at work at a restaurant in New York City when someone ran in yelling that the Japs had bombed the Pearl Harbor Navy Base. Joe, like most everyone, didn't know where Pearl Harbor was. Someone ran to get a radio. Someone else ran to get a map. Soon everyone, workers and customers, gathered around the radio listening to the reports.

The next day the restaurant had the radio on at noon to hear Roosevelt's speech. He was scheduled to speak to a joint session of congress at 12:30. At that time, everyone was around the radio, with no orders being prepared or cooked by the workers during the speech.

In August 1941, the US had imposed a trade embargo on Japan because of their military aggression in China. The US demanded that Japan withdraw troops from China. Japan imported 80% if its oil from the US. With US oil cut off, Japan wanted the oil in Indonesia and Malaysia, and attacked the US naval base to prevent the US from interfering with the Japanese conquest of Southeast Asia.

Very soon young men started to line up to enlist. Draft boards started drafting men. Joe's brother, Mike, enlisted for the duration of the war in April 1942, followed by Andy in September. Joe knew that his draft notice would be coming soon. Both brothers wrote him and told him that he ought to enlist in the Navy, because he would see less combat action in the Navy then he would in the Army. So in February 1943, just before his twentieth birthday, taking his brothers' advice, he enlisted in the Navy for the duration of the war.

Now Walter and Dorotha had three sons in the war. Walter listened to the radio daily for war news. At Stanley's someone would always be reading the newspaper to those gathered at the beer garden. Dorotha went to church every day to pray for her sons and light a prayer candle. Their son Jacob was working for Bethlehem Steel and had children, so he was told he would not be drafted because his job was important to the war cause.

Posters encouraging sacrifice and support for the war effort began to appear everywhere – "Buy bonds"; "Uncle Sam wants you"; "Donate old Metal items". Many items were rationed – meat, cheese, butter, lard, coffee, sugar, silk, nylon, shoes, and gas for example. Families were issued blue ration booklets. Stores gave change for ration stamps, with tokens; giving red point tokens as change for red stamps (for meat and butter), and blue point tokens for blue stamps (processed foods). The tokens were made of compressed wood fiber, the size of dimes. People were asked to donate old nylons and stockings for use in parachutes and ropes, and tin and steel for scrap and metal drives. Retail stores, city halls, and post offices were collection centers.

Walter had taken a job at the mine weighing the coal carts. He was too old at 62 to mine coal anymore, getting winded too easily with his black lung disease. He would take a metal flask of water with a little bit of brandy or wine in it to drink if he started to wheeze to help relax his lungs. It was an old miner's home remedy for lung ailments that they kept in their pocket. He made less money as a weigh master, so Mike and Joe had their military allotment sent to Walter and Dorotha. Andy had gotten married when on a leave, and his allotment went to his new wife who was soon pregnant.

Joe was sent to Norfolk Naval Base for boot camp. During boot camp all sailors with 20-20 vision were given more eye sight testing. Those with better than 20-20 vision were assigned to Navigation and Lookout training after boot camp.

Three weeks into the training, many in the class were told they would finish training on the new USS New Jersey battleship.

When they arrived at the Philadelphia shipyard, they were told to leave their duffle bags on the bus and form a line on deck. Soon they were passing mattresses from man to man down stairs to the lower decks, putting a mattress on each bunk. The bunks were three high in six and a half foot high sleeping areas.

After the mattress duty, the crew had to unload boxes of food so the cooks could start cooking their meals. Next, the crew retrieved their duffle bags and picked up sheets and pillow for their assigned bunk. They had to follow procedure as to where each item was to go in their locker. The next morning, they had to be in their dress uniforms and standing at attention for the commissioning of the USS New Jersey. It was May 23, 1943. The first crew on a ship were called plankers. These plankers had a melting pot of names – English, German, Irish, Italian, Jewish, Eastern European, and other nationalities. Some were first generation American-born like Joe, some were born in other countries.

The next week, the New Jersey started its maiden voyage down the Chesapeake to Norfolk Naval Base. Their training continued over the next few months in the Atlantic and Caribbean. In December, Joe was promoted to seaman first class. Each promotion meant more money. Now he was making $66 per month instead of $54. He also got a seven day leave in December, so he would be home for Christmas. During

World War II, all active duty military had to be in uniform at all times, even when on leave.

While on leave, Joe and a couple of friends, also on leave, drove around visiting friends in his friend Max's dad's car. One day they went to a billiard parlor in Forty Fort. While they were playing pool, some girls were waiting for a table to open, so Joe invited them to play with him and his two friends. The girls accepted. Two soldiers and a sailor in uniforms attracted the girls. Joe, with his wavy black hair and big smile, talked to the girls between turns.

An hour later the girls said they needed to get home. One girl, a 17 year old named Dot, short with dark hair and greenish blue eyes, offered to write Joe while he was in the Pacific, which was where the New Jersey was headed at the first of the year. All the crew knew was that they were headed to the Pacific, nothing more precise than that. But nobody had a pencil and paper to write down addresses.

"Why don't I come by your house with my service address tomorrow night," Joe offered.

"Okay, come by tomorrow at seven," Dot offered. "I'll be on the front porch. Fifty Butler, here in Forty Fort."

"See you then."

The next evening, Joe walked to the house in Forty Fort. As he walked up the street he could see Dot sitting on the porch with her parents, a younger sister, and a young man in an army uniform.   The neighborhood was middle class, much nicer and larger houses than in Swoyersville. Homes had cars parked in front or in driveways.

Dot introduced Joe to her parents, sister, and brother who was home on leave. Her dad shook hands with Joe, but did not get up or smile. Her brother smiled and got up to shake hands.

"Where are you stationed?" her brother asked.

"Norfolk, battleship New Jersey, until we sail in a week and a half," Joe responded.

"Where to?" the brother asked.

"Somewhere in the Pacific," Joe answered. "How about you?"

"I ship out to California in a week."

"Come on Joe, let's go for a walk," Dot suggested. "They'll talk all night to you if I don't take you away."

They talked while they walked down the sidewalk, Dot waving to neighbors sitting on their front porches.

"You have a nice house, it's big," Joe commented. "What does your dad do?"

"He's a metallurgist for Vulcan Iron Works," she told him. "But with seven kids money doesn't go too far. Now my older sister is living here with her three kids, because her husband is in the marines in the Pacific."

"It must be crowded in the house."

"Not really, my other two brothers are in the service also. One is a Navy Officer in Washington State. Maybe you will meet him sometime. The other is in the Coast Guard in Florida. My other older sister is in Kansas where her husband is stationed in the Army. So that just leaves me, my little sister and my older sister with her three children. How many at your parent's house?"

"I'm the youngest," Joe answered. "So no kids live at the house now, just my parents. But three of us are home on leave right now. It made my parents happy. Two of my brothers are in the army. My oldest brother works in the steel mill in Bethlehem and has kids so they won't be drafting him."

"Do you have any sisters?" Dot asked.

"Yes, two sisters," he said. "They're both married and live in Philadelphia."

"It's so hard on the parents, having sons in the war," Dot commented.

Joe noticed the stars hanging in the windows of the homes. Dot's parents had a small flag with three blue stars in their window, as did his parents. It was tradition for parents to put a small red, white and blue banner with a blue star for each son in the war in the front window. A gold star meant a son died in the war. They passed one house that had a flag with one gold star. Joe stopped. "They lost someone," he observed.

"Yes," Dot said sadly. "It's so sad. They have four daughters and only one son and he died in the war. Shot down over Europe. He was a friend of my brothers. They played ball together."

"The Nazis and the Japs won't last long and we'll win and the war will end soon, you'll see," Joe said.

"But how many neighbors will not be coming home before it ends?" Dot observed. "You take care of yourself, Joe."

"Don't worry about me. Our battleship is the largest in the world, almost 900 feet long. The guns are the largest. When we were in the ocean practicing we hit targets thirty miles away."

"You can't see that far."

"I'm in the lookout company. With my binoculars I can see that far from the highest lookout post on the ship, which is higher than the bridge. The Japs are going to run when they see us coming."

"I hope so."

When they got back to her house, they exchanged addresses. Her family was in the house listening to the radio.

"I take the train back to Norfolk tomorrow, and we ship out very soon," Joe told her. "I'll write you first chance I get.

Of course you won't know where I am. I won't be able to tell you. Just the Pacific."

"I'll watch for the New Jersey in the newspaper."

"Save some articles for me."

"I will," Dot said. "And I'll write next week."

As Joe left and walked down the street, he smiled as he heard Dot's little sister say loudly, "he's handsome."

On January 7, 1944 the New Jersey passed through the Panama Canal on its way to join the 5th fleet at the Ellice Islands, located 2,600 miles southwest of Hawaii. The fleet consisted of carriers, battleships, cruisers, destroyers and submarines.

Starting on January 29, the New Jersey participated in attacks in the Marshall Islands, north of the Ellice Islands. On February 4 the New Jersey became the Flagship of Admiral Spruance.

The New Jersey took part in a surface engagement with the Japanese fleet on February 16, sinking a destroyer and a trawler. Joe witnessed many ships firing shells the size of bombs at each other. He could feel the vibrations of the massive guns against his body. He saw many planes firing at enemy ships and planes.

He was thankful that he had communication ear phones when on the lookout post, thereby deafening the loud sound of the massive guns. Through the noise he had to listen to the chatter on his earphones in case his post was being given instructions or was questioned. Joe tried not to let it show how frightened he was.

The Fleet was constantly on the move. With it on the move, the Japanese Navy couldn't keep track of their whereabouts. The planes of the fleet were constantly on the lookout for Jap ships. The fleet was responsible to bombard islands prior to marine landings.

In March, the New Jersey bombarded Japanese shore batteries on Mille Atoll in the Marshall Islands. In April, the New Jersey screened the carriers' striker force for the invasion of Aitape, and Hollandia, New Guinea, 2,000 miles southwest of the Marshalls. From there they participated in shore bombardment of Ponape Island, 1,000 miles northeast of New Guinea, destroying fuel tanks, damaging the airfield, and demolishing Japanese headquarters.

The lookout company had to communicate with the bridge about enemy aircraft approaching, if a target had been hit and how to correct if it hadn't, and the distance to a planned target. Joe was usually on the highest part of the ship, higher than the bridge. After three months in battle, Joe thought about what his brothers said about going into the Navy and seeing less action. "I've seen more action in one day than my two Army brothers have seen so far in the war," Joe wrote to his brothers and Dot without disclosing any locations. He didn't write this to his parents. He didn't want them to worry.

In June, the New Jersey participated in the Battle of Saipan, north of Ponape, then the Battle of the Philippine Sea, far west of Saipan. The battleship screened carriers, as three Jap carriers were sunk by submarines and planes during the battle. The Japs lost over 400 planes, with the US losing only seventeen.

July found the New Jersey participating in the Battle of Guam and Palau, 1,500 miles east of the Philippines, then heading to Pearl Harbor. On August 9, the New Jersey became the flagship of Admiral Halsey of the third fleet while at Pearl Harbor. Joe and some other shipmates got an eight hour pass one day while at Pearl Harbor. They got their picture taken with Hawaiian girls in grass skirts at a souvenir shop. The stop at Pearl Harbor was short lived, as the New Jersey participated in strikes on various Japanese held Philippine Islands in September and October.

One day in September, the bridge couldn't see an island that they were to bomb. Joe was on the highest lookout post with another lookout. "We can see it," Joe communicated back to the bridge. "Well I can't see it," someone from the bridge called back. "It's there," Joe replied.

A minute later they saw Admiral Halsey climbing the ladder to their post. "Give me those damned binoculars," Halsey said when he squeezed on the lookout stand.

"Straight that way, sir" Joe said pointing.

"I still don't see it," Halsey argued.

"With all do respects, sir, lookouts have better than 20-20 vision," Joe tried to explain. "With these binoculars we can see further this high off the water, further than your more mature eyes."

"Are you saying I'm too old to see," Halsey objected as he stared Joe in the eye.

"All I'm saying is that these guns can shoot that far," Joe explained further. "Those islands are within range. The bridge said it should be the right island. You can have a spotter plane from a nearby carrier confirm."

"That island has anti-aircraft artillery," Halsey informed. "If we can hit the island now from here, let's do it and the spotter plane can tell us if we hit it without getting too close."

"I agree, sir," Joe said even though he didn't think his opinion mattered much.

"Tell the bridge to fire," Halsey ordered.

Halsey left the lookout post, and a minute later, the big 16" massive guns started firing. Seconds after that, Joe could see explosions, meaning they were hitting land and not water. Soon he heard the spotter plane radio the ship that Jap gun placements were being hit, and it looked like some ammo storage had been hit as well, causing massive damage.

A half hour later the bridge told Joe and his fellow lookout that the Admiral said to tell them, "Good Job." Fighter bombers attacked the island next with little resistance. Marines would be landing the next morning.

The next month Joe got promoted to Coxswain (petty officer third class). He wrote home the good news. It meant more in his pay, as he was now making $78 per month. Dot wrote him almost every week. The ship didn't get mail often, and he would sometimes receive three of her letters at once, so he would look at the post mark first, then read them in order.

In the fall of 1944, US ships started to experience Jap kamikaze planes. Joe couldn't believe it, as Jap pilots aimed their planes directly into the ships, as if they were a bomb itself. Anti-aircraft gunners had to shoot down the plane before it reached them. One plane just missed Joe and another lookout, its wing chopping a piece of the radar above them. It looked like the Jap pilot tried to pull the plane back up, but his now damaged wing kept him from creating lift, and the plane skimmed the surface of the ocean causing it to tumble over several times until it sank.

Joe always went to church service on Sunday. Times varied so that if you were on duty, a sailor could go at a different time. The exception was during combat, when everyone was on duty. After the kamikaze attack, Joe went to the chaplain when he got off duty.

"Why would anyone want to commit suicide like these kamikazes?" Joe asked the chaplain.

"Theirs is not a Christian religion," the Chaplain tried to explain. "We cherish every life. The Japanese schools are run by the military, and they are taught it is an honor to die for Japan. So that may be part of their military mindset. I really don't know. I've read that, as soldiers, they must be willing to die for the emperor."

"Such a waste of life," Joe commented. "At the same time they are going to run out of pilots and planes."

"That will speed up the end of the war," the Chaplain wished. "I know you pray, Joe, this is a good time to reflect in prayer. Let's pray." Joe sat in the ship's chapel and prayed silently.

After talking to the chaplain, Joe bought a pack of cigarettes at the ship's store for a nickel, and went on deck to sit in a designated smoking area that was always filled with off duty smokers. Joe sat with a fresh breeze blowing across his face. He had started smoking in New York and smoked more in the Navy. It was a cheap habit in the Navy. During training when a superior said take a smoke break, you did.

The New Jersey participated in the second Battle of the Philippine Sea, then in mid-December the fleet found itself in a furious typhoon which sank three US destroyers. The larger New Jersey came through undamaged, but rough seas tossed it about like a toy boat in a tub. Joe held on to his bunk with both hands, as objects and people not attached to something were tossed about. Joe was even more frightened than when the kamikaze missed him. The plane was over quickly, but the typhoon lasted for hours, almost the entire day. Sailors were throwing up and grabbing on to whatever they could. They were glad that they were on the larger battleship, then on a smaller destroyer. They were confident their ship would make it despite the frightening rollercoaster ride.

The New Jersey continued to participate in support of air strikes on Okinawa, north of the Philippines; Formosa, west of Okinawa; and Luzon, Philippines. In February 1945, the New Jersey participated in the support of attacks on Iwo Jima, 800 miles east of Okinawa. March found the New Jersey back to bombarding Okinawa, followed by strikes on other islands and southern mainland Japan.

#######

In August 1944, the Germans resumed deporting Jews from Slovakia to concentration camps in Poland. Vasil and Mikolas went to their Jewish friend in a nearby town to help him change his shop sign and hide any signs of him being Jewish. He and his family changed their names and told customers to call them by new temporary Christian names. They boxed up any symbols that they were Jewish and placed Christian bibles and crucifixes around their shop and home. The box of Jewish items was hidden in the attic for a day in the near future. The family even wore necklaces with crosses.

"Thank you for letting me borrow your Christian items, Vasil," the man thanked him. "I hope it is only for a short time until I can return them. God bless you."

"Do you think this will work?" Vasil asked his friend.

"I hope and pray. If we were in a large city with a Jewish neighborhood, the German Army would tell the police to round up Jews. If the police do not, the Germans shoot them."

"Fear controls everyone," Vasil observed. "People fear that by not reporting where Jews are, will get them shot. Everyone is afraid. If Slovakia doesn't do what the Germans tell them to do, the Germans will just take over the country completely like they did in Austria and Czech. Our leaders in Bratislava would turn in their own mothers if it served their own interests."

"If this was a mostly Jewish town, the Germans would make the Slovak Army help them round up Jews," the Jew pointed out. "But there are few of us Jews in this Christian town. This town only has one Constable and he is my friend. He will be quiet and say he knows of no Jews in town. We Jews will stop going to the Jewish village where the synagogue is until the evil is gone. We will blend in. The evil Nazis will eventually be overcome."

"I hope it works," Vasil wished. "There is always the danger of someone turning you in. I will pray for you."

On their way home that day, Vasil and Mikolas noticed two boys climbing one of their apple trees as they approached home.

"Those apple trees aren't quite ready for picking yet," Vasil noted.

"I hope it doesn't give them a belly ache," Mikolas said.

"I doubt it. They'll be fine. I wonder whose boys they are."

"Nobody I know."

When Mikolas drove the horse and wagon to the barn the boys looked like they were trying to hide. Vasil walked over to the apple trees. The boys hid behind a tree trunk. "Hello, do you need a drink of water to wash down those apples?" Vasil yelled to the boys.

The taller boy stuck his head from behind the trunk. "Drink?" he asked in Polish. Vasil said water in Polish.

"Ya," the boy said. Vasil waved his arm for them to follow him.

They came out from behind the tree each carrying a suitcase. They were dirty like they hadn't washed in a week. Their clothes looked like they had been worn for a week straight. Their hats were soiled and they wore coats in warm weather.

Living close to Poland, most people in Osturna knew some Polish. Vasil invited them into the house and Kate got them each a glass of water, which they drank quickly.

"Would you like some milk?" Kate asked in Polish.

"Ya," they both said. She also got them some potato bread and butter.

"Where are you from?" Vasil asked.'

"Up north," the older one answered

"Where are you going?" Vasil asked.

"Away from the Germans," the older one explained.

"That might be a long walk," Vasil observed. "Although the further south you go the better chance to stay away from them." Vasil suspected that maybe they might be Jewish, trying avoid being sent to a concentration camp. "Sometimes the best way to avoid your enemies is to blend in with the surroundings."

"How?" the older one asked.

"Well, I know a shopkeeper who is Jewish who has packed up anything that would hint he is Jewish," Vasil explained. "He now wears a Christian cross necklace and has an Orthodox Christian bible on his counter at his shop. His shop sign now has a Christian name on it as proprietor, and has his customers call him by that Christian name. So if Germans come by, or someone assisting the Germans, they won't be suspicious."

As Vasil spoke, they ate bread and butter as if they hadn't had much to eat in a while. By now, Mikolas and his siblings also sat at the table.

"You can stay for supper," Kate offered. "But you must tell me your names and where you are from and how old you are."

"I am Jakub Klaczko," the older one said. "We are from Cracow. I am fourteen."

"I am Menachem," the young one said with a high voice. "I am twelve."

"That is a girl's name," Kate observed.

Menachem took her hat off and her hair fell down to her shoulders. "Pants and a hat are more practical when walking through the woods and mountains," she said.

"Where are your parents?" Kate asked said softly, not wanting to excite the two children.

Jakub looked around the table at everyone, not knowing if he could trust these people. A look around the room told him that these people were not Jewish.

"We won't tell anyone what you tell us," Vasil said slowly.

Finally Jakub spoke. "The Germans came and took away my parents. My dad hid us in the coal bin in the cellar. After a couple of days we left heading south into the mountains. Our food is gone now. We were hoping to find an empty house near farms, where we could hide, where we can help harvest food for money or food."

"Well, harvest time is here," Vasil suggested. "There is an empty room next door at Kate's parent's house. Mikolas stays at their house," pointing at Mikolas. "If you want to stay hiding here for a little while, I will talk to Kate's father. First we need to give you temporary Christian names so no one will be suspicious." He looked at the boy. "You Jakub will be Jake Kovac, and Menachem we will call you Marya."

"While Vasil is talking to my parents, you two can take a bath and we will wash your clothes," Kate ordered. "We will tell the neighbors you are cousins from Poland here to help us with the harvest. While you are here, you will go to church with us, so you will appear to be like cousins. You can go back to being Jewish sometime in the future."

"The Germans are going to self-destruct in the future," Mikolas added. "Should the Germans come through town, you can hide in the woods."

Jakub shared Mikolas's room, and Menachem was put in the spare room in Mikel and Anna's home. Menachem was a big help to Anna, as she was unable to get around without a cane.

In September 1944, a Slovak Resistance Army was forming to fight the Germans. Mikolas, now 24, and several of his friends left Osturna to join the Resistance, despite Kate's objections. The young men took their hunting rifles or shotguns with them when they wen to join the unit, as they had been instructed.

After a few weeks of training, the resistance militia assisted a Soviet brigade in driving the Germans back through Slovakia during October. The militia helped by resupplying troops on the front with ammo they would unload from trucks. They also passed out food to the troops and even dug latrines when needed.

The Germans were unable to send more troops or supplies to Slovakia, as they had enough problems with the Soviets driving them out of Poland, and the Americans and British driving them out of France. In December, Mikolas and the Resistance fighters assisted the Soviets in the Battle of Budapest. On December 26, 1944, the Russian and Romanian Armies surrounded Budapest, which was defended by Hungarian and German Armies. Mikolas was assigned to move artillery shells from the trucks and stack them next to artillery guns. As the guns fired it was so loud that he wrapped a cloth around his head to cover his ears. With shrapnel flying everywhere, Mikolas grabbed a helmet from a dead soldier to wear. The freezing temperature effected both sides. Mikolas took a coat off a taller dead soldier and put it on over his coat in an attempt to try to warm up.

Everyone was asking for food. An officer assigned Mikolas and another soldier to butcher frozen horse carcasses they found on the streets. With a shortage of trucks and other equipment, horses had been put into good use. They would pick a dead one that had recently been killed by shrapnel; dead long enough to start freezing, but fresh enough not to have turned bad. After butchering, they would start a fire to cook the meat. Soldiers would line up when they started to smell the cooking. They would put a bucket full of snow next to the fire to melt, so soldiers would have water to drink.

One day, Mikolas saw a bakery shop with its door blown to pieces. He walked in to discover no one inside, but plenty of flour stacked on a shelf. The ovens were undamaged. He asked around and found a couple of militia soldiers who were bakers. Soon they had bread to go with the horse meat and melted snow.

On one especially cold day, Mikolas saw Demjam, a Slovak he had befriended, going into a sewer. "Why are you going in there?" Mikolas asked him.

"The water is frozen in there, but it is not as cold as out here," Demjam Djurkan answered. "No wind."

"Doesn't it smell?" Mikolas asked.

"Yes, but our noses are too cold to smell. But it is worth it because we can get to other parts of the city without being seen and pop up and surprise the Germans," Demjam continued. "Only problem is, the Germans are doing the same, so you have to be careful."

"You do need a flashlight, don't you?" Mikolas asked.

"Yes, but we found some at a store that had the front blown in and no one there," he confessed.

"I think I will stick to the cooking assignment, so I'm next to the fire," Mikolas said.

"What are you cooking?" Demjam asked.

"A horse," Mikolas replied. "Should have some ready in about 30 minutes. And a friend is baking some bread in an oven around the corner."

"The Germans can wait," Demjam smiled. "I'll eat first. Let me help you." Demjam stayed the next week with Mikolas and his butchers and bakers, helping by riding a live horse each day to the outskirts of the city to steal a cow, or goat, or lamb, and bring it walking back on a rope for the butchers.

As the Russians advanced, they came upon an ammo factory that was still producing bullets. The Russians took anything that would fit their guns and told the workers not to stop working, and send the bill to the war department in Moscow.

In February, Hungarian soldiers started to defect and fight on the Soviet side. On February 13, 1945 the Germans finally surrendered. Eighty percent of Budapest's buildings were destroyed or damaged. After the German surrender the Slovak militia headed back to Bratislava, Presov, and other Slovakia cities to protect those areas. Mikolas and Demjam were assigned to Presov which was fortunate as Demjam's village was only 20 kilometers from Presov. Mikolas got invited several times to the Djurkan family home for delicious Slovak meals. They would take a train most of the way. Demjam's father, Vaskos, told them stories from his experiences in World War I. When Vaskos found out what village Mikolas was from, he said "I had a good friend in the war from Osturna. His name was Vasil."

"My dad's name is Vasil," Mikolas said. "Vasil Smolenak."

"Yes, that is him," Vaskos exclaimed. "He was here in Klemburk dining with my family also. You must tell your father about us meeting."

"Of course," Mikolas agreed. "Do you have a phone? My parents have a phone now. We can call."

They called, surprising Vasil and Kate who were excited to find that their son was fine. Vasil and Vaskos reminisced about old times. Vasil made Vaskos promise to come to Osturna to visit during hunting season.

The victories of 1945 brought about the reestablishment of Czechoslovakia in April 1945, and Slovakia was no longer independent from the Czech half. Days later the Germans surrendered to the Allies and the European war was over.

Days before the German surrender, Mikolas headed home. As he approached home the winds from the mountains brought the pleasing smell of trees and flowers, refreshing the air like a promise of better life ahead.

Mikolas arrived home the day before the radio announced the formal surrender of Germany. Kate and Vasil were quick to help organize a village celebration to welcome home the resistance fighters and the end of the war.

Vasil was glad to have his hunting rifle back. "We will put that hunting rifle to good use and go hunting," Vasil told Mikolas. "But first let's go party."

"You will have to dance with the girls for me," Mikel weakly said as he sat in a wheelchair holding his cane. He was now 94 and still had all his hair, now all white.

"Gladly grandpa," Mikolas said. "I'll push you to the party."

"No you won't," Mikel corrected. "You have those girls push me. They're prettier than you."

Jakub and Menachem had been staying at the Vascura house for over eight months. The neighbors knew them as Jake and Marya, cousins from a Polish village. At the celebration party at St Michaels, Jake asked Vasil if he could tell everyone he was Jewish and explain why he must leave the next week.

"It's entirely up to you," Vasil said. "You two have been a great help to Kate's parents. We will all be sorry to see you go. I know you must go find your parents. I will take you two in the wagon to the train station and buy you two tickets to Cracow.

"I will pay you back," Jakub said.

"No, I owe it to you two for all your help." Vasil asked for everyone's attention and told them that Jakub had something he wanted to tell everyone.

"My real name is Jakub Klaczko and this is my sister Menachem," Jakub said. "We are Jewish from Cracow. Our parents were taken by the Germans to a concentration camp. My sister and I hid in the woods, then headed south to this nice village where the Vascuras and Smolenaks let us stay. We are grateful to them and this village for helping us survive. Now we must go home to find our parents."

Ladies went up to Jakub and Menachem hugging the youngsters and offering help. The next day villagers showed up at the Vascura house with food, clothes, and money for their trip. The priest and his wife came and blessed them, that they may have a safe journey.

A few days later, Mikolas went with Vasil to take them to the train station. On the way they saw an abandoned German Army truck in a ditch on the side of the road.

After saying good bye to Jakub and Menachem at the train, Vasil bought a rope at a hardware store, and headed to the abandoned truck. To their surprise the key was in the ignition and the truck started. They attached the rope to the front bumper, and unhooked the horse harness from the wagon and attached it to the rope. Vasil put the truck in gear and stepped on the gas as the two horses pulled at Mikolas's command. Slowly, the truck spun its wheels as it climbed out of the ditch as the horses pulled. The truck ran out of gas on the way home, so Vasil stayed by the truck until Mikolas came back with gas. They had had a large filled gas can in the barn to refill their tractor. A couple weeks later after a new paint job and some mechanical work they had a good farm truck.

#######

Late in the day on April 12, 1945, the Captain of the USS New Jersey announced that President Roosevelt had died. The chaplain then said a prayer. Later, the captain announced that Truman was sworn in as the new President.

"Truman?" Joe asked another sailor. "I never heard of him before he became vice president. Roosevelt was the only

President I ever knew. I was only ten when he became President. My dad will be so upset. He really liked Roosevelt. Voted for him every time."

"My dad too," the other sailor said. "He even put a sign in our yard before every election – vote for Roosevelt."

Later that month, the New Jersey went east to Puget Sound Naval Shipyard in Washington for an overhaul. As a result, Joe was given a 20 day leave. He caught a troop train headed across the country. As the steam train approached some small town stations to take on water and coal, the townspeople would be waiting with sandwiches and music in the depot. Even though the train may only be there 20 minutes, soldiers and sailors would jump off the train and dance with one of the young ladies while eating a sandwich with one hand. The town would receive word ahead of time that a troop train was coming, so townsfolk could bring the food and dance records.

There was not enough time for a letter to home when he found out that he had the leave, so he sent two short telegrams before boarding the train, one to his parents, and one to Dot:

"Battleship docked West Coast. Coming home on leave. Joe."

During World War II families were informed by telegram of a military killed-in-action or missing-in-action. When

Dorotha saw the telegram delivery person arrive on a bicycle and knock on her door, she screamed, "Is it one of my boys?"

The young man saw the worried look on her face. "Don't worry, it's good," he said.

Dot's mother had a similar reaction to a telegram arriving, having three sons in the war also. "Joe?" she asked, then realizing the telegram was addressed to her daughter. When Dot got home from work, she told her mom, "You remember the cute sailor you met and I have been writing."

Joe was happy to be home, no crowded crew quarters, no crowded train, no loud explosions, and no Jap aircraft firing at him. When he got to his house, after hugging his parents, he ran through the garden that had been freshly planted, small plants sprouting. He sat at the end of the yard and looked out across the pond and listened to the quiet, interrupted by the occasional chicken clucking or pig squealing.

As Joe sat there, he thought he heard a phone ring. It sounded like it was coming from their house. He heard his dad talking to someone. When he got back in the house Joe asked, "Did you get a phone? I need to use it when you are off dad." It was a neighbor on the phone asking if the rumor was true that Joe was home.

Dot squealed when Joe called her. "When are you coming over?" she asked.

"Tomorrow, my parents are throwing an impromptu neighborhood party tonight. They're setting out chairs on the side yard. They called a lot of people. Several are bringing musical instruments."

"We will do the same thing here tomorrow at my house, so be here at 6," she informed him. "My one brother is home on leave from the Coast Guard. You two will be the guests of honor."

"I'll be there," he promised.

Dot had been saving newspaper articles of the USS New Jersey in a photo album. She also saved articles about any soldier or sailor she or her family knew. Unfortunately some of these articles were obituaries.

Kossack St celebrated with guitars, harmonicas, and accordions. The sailor got kissed and hugged and toasted. Joe danced with any girl that would. He preferred the polka, but didn't mind a slow dance with a cute girl.

The next evening at Dot's house, the party didn't have to be in the yard as her parent's house had plenty of room in the living room, dining room and front porch. A piano was in the corner next to a phonograph. Her parents sat on the porch watching, not like Joe's parents who were part of the party dancing, and talking to everyone. Swing music of the early 40's were the most popular records played. No one had a polka record at this party. Less hugging and kissing of the boys home on leave, than at Joe's parent's home. Joe did manage to hold

Dot tightly when they danced a slow dance. At the end of the party Joe wanted to kiss her goodbye, but with her parents sitting there, he was reluctant.

"Are you going to ask me out to a movie?" Dot asked him before he left.

"How about tomorrow evening," Joe asked, taking the hint. After they agreed on a time, she pecked him on the cheek and he did the same.

When walked down her street the next day to take her to the movie, car horns were honking, people were cheering on their porches, and radios were turned on very load. He could hear a radio announcer saying that the Germans had surrendered. Dot hugged him, as did her mom and sister as they celebrated. Over the past several days various German armies had been surrendering, but now the Germans had signed an unconditional surrender of all German forces. The European War was over.

They saw each other several times before he left to return to Puget Sound. On his way to the west coast he stopped at Chicago for a day to visit cousins and aunts and uncles. Every male cousin in his twenties was in the war in one service or another.

Joe never used foul language, never cussed or swore, a rarity after over two years in the Navy. Instead of cussing Joe had some sayings to use instead. He might call someone a "bald-headed Elmer". The newspapers had a comic called Elmer Fudd who was a bald-headed character.

When Joe returned from leave, a chief petty officer told him to go to the high lookout post. Joe went to the ladder and started climbing when he realized that the ladder had no lookout post at the top of it anymore. It just led to the new larger radar and was now just a service ladder. Then he noticed a new ladder nearby that led to a new lookout stand not as high as the old one.

The chief and several others started laughing as Joe looked around at the changes. "You bald headed Elmer," Joe yelled, scratching his head.

On July 4th 1945, they set sail for California, where the New Jersey went through training exercises for the benefit of some new crew members before heading to Pearl Harbor on the 19th. Upon arriving at Pearl Harbor, Joe and others got shore leave once, between more training exercises.

They were cruising to Guam, when on August 7, the Captain announced that a large atomic bomb had been dropped the day before on Hiroshima, Japan, destroying most of the city. "Hopefully this will bring us closer to the end of the war," the Captain concluded.

"What's an atomic bomb?" Joe asked another sailor.

"A big one evidently," the sailor answered.

"How many bombs did he say?" someone asked.

"I think just one," Joe said. "It's hard to believe that one bomb can destroy most of a city."

Three days later the Captain announced that another atomic bomb had been dropped the previous day, this time on Nagasaki, Japan.

On August 13th the New Jersey anchored off the harbor of Guam awaiting orders as to where to join up with a fleet. But on August 15th, President Truman announced the surrender of the Japanese. When the ship loud speaker announced this, everyone stopped what they were doing and started yelling, jumping, dancing, and throwing hats in the air. Joe knew now that it was just of matter of time when his enlistment would be up.

The New Jersey was now assigned to the Fifth fleet under Admiral Spruance. They set sail for Manilla, anchoring on August 21. Many Japanese merchant ships and war ships were buried in the harbor, their rusted masts and structures jutting above the water. Hardly a building in Manilla wasn't damaged.

On August 28th the New Jersey headed to Okinawa, anchoring on the 30th with many other ships of the fifth and seventh fleets. With the navy point system, Joe had many points for all the combat his ship had been in. Being he was a planker (first crew on a new ship) he had all the ship's points. Those with the most points got to go home first.

On August 30th the US troops started landing in Japan to occupy the country. With the New Jersey in Okinawa and the USS Missouri battleship already outside Tokyo harbor, the decision was made to have the signing of the surrender on the Missouri. President Truman was from Missouri, so despite the New Jersey having been in more combat action, the Missouri would do the honors of holding the ceremony on its deck on September 2nd.

This upset the crew of the New Jersey. "We deserved the honor having been an admiral's flagship for much of the war and having been in so much combat," Joe wrote home. The crew grumbled and complained all the way to Tokyo harbor, arriving on September 17th and serving as the flagship of Naval Forces in Japan.

At the end of September, the crew were allowed 8 hour daylight passes to go ashore and shop in Tokyo. It was felt that the devastated economy would be helped by sailors and soldiers spending money for souvenirs or other items. Joe, like many others sailors, was afraid of Jap army snipers in hiding, not wanting to surrender, taking pot shots at a US uniform, so he declined.

In early October Joe's company commander called him to his office. "Wascura, you have an excellent record and seven battle stars on your ribbons," the officer said. "Did you ever consider making the navy a career?"

Joe, being friendly and jovial, was not fond of military command style. He didn't like the crew's cussing or using the lord's name in vain. "No sir, I would prefer to just go home," Joe replied.

"If you re-up for three years, you would get promoted to petty officer second class," the officer pointed out. "That is more money. I'm only recommending the best to re-up. You would be stationed in the states."

"Thank you for the offer, sir," Joe said. "But I'll take my chances at getting a good job at home."

"Very well. In a few months, if you change your mind, you can always come back. You'll be leaving next week. You will catch a Navy Transport plane at the Tokyo airport. After several plane transfers, you'll catch a train on the west coast to Norfolk Naval Base where you will be separated from the Navy. It will all be in your orders. Good Luck."

Joe's smile was ear to ear as he shook the officer's hand. Those with the most points got a choice of a new assignment in the states if they reenlisted, or being among the first to leave the military.

Joe didn't send a telegram this time. He wanted to surprise everyone. After he got his discharge papers in Norfolk, Joe took the train to Wilkes-Barre, then the bus to near Kossack St. He walked down the street, duffle bag over his shoulder, grinning from ear to ear. It was late afternoon and Dorotha would be starting to prepare supper for Walter.

The winds from the mountains brought the cool clear smell of falling leaves and evergreen trees, refreshing the air, like a promise of better life ahead.

Joe walked around the back door and tossed his duffle bag on the floor. Dorotha turned, startled by the noise, "Joe," she yelled.

After squeezing the slender but muscular Joe, she asked, "Are you home for good now?"

"Yes mom. These are my discharge papers," he said as he pulled the papers out of his pocket.

"I'm so happy you are safe and home," she cried wiping happy tears. "Now no more wars. The bad Nazis and Japs are no more. Peace here for good. Now let me feed you. You are skinny."

"Amen," Joe agreed. "Where's dad?"

"Oh you know. He always stops at the beer garden on the way home from the mine."

"I'll go surprise him," Joe said as he opened the ice box for something to drink. "Why don't you get an electric refrigerator? Think of all the money you would save not having to buy blocks of ice."

"With war rationing, they weren't available. With the war over now, they will be available. But maybe we should wait. Your father is going to retire in the spring. But the social security and miners' pension will not be as much as what he makes now."

"Well, with me getting a job, and the money I've been saving and the money you have been saving, we can get the refrigerator and an electric stove too. You would save on coal."

"I hope you boys can find jobs. With the war over, all the factories are stopping making planes and tanks. The mines are expecting a slowdown. Your dad heard they might be going to three or four days per week next month."

"Don't worry, the factories will be making refrigerators, stoves, clothes washers, and cars. They will have to hire workers."

After he ate some food, Joe headed to the beer garden. As he entered the beer garden Joe yelled, "I'll have a beer."

Walter, sitting at the bar with other miners, turned at the sound of the familiar voice. "Joe," he yelled as he jumped off the stool, arms spread out for a hug from the sailor.

"Put his beer on my tab," Walter told the bartender as they sat at the bar.

"Nonsense," the bartender said. "It's on the house. Welcome home boy."

"How long you got leave for?" Walter asked.

"I'm out. With all the ribbons with battle stars, I had many points," Joe said as he pointing to the ribbons with stars on his uniform.

"Wonderful, son."

"What's this rank?" the bartender asked pointing to Joe's sleeve.

"Coxswain," Joe answered. "Same as third class petty officer."

"Got promoted from seaman second class to first class to Coxswain," Walter bragged proudly. "I bet in another two years he'd be a commander if he stayed in."

"I don't know about that," Joe laughed.

"Mike's Army company is being transferred from England to New Jersey this week," Walter filled Joe in on his brothers' statuses. "He thinks he will be discharged after the first of the year. Andy's Army unit is being sent from the Philippines to the stateside very soon. He thinks he will be discharged after the first of the year also. You know he got a Purple Heart because he got scratched by shrapnel in the hip. He healed in a few days."

"A toast to Andy's wound," Joe said holding up his beer.

Everyone in the bar yelled, "To Andy," and lifted their mugs.

That evening after supper, Joe headed out to Forty Fort to see Dot. Joe didn't call her first. She was sitting on the front porch with her younger sister and her parents. She could see the Navy uniform coming down the sidewalk. When she realized it was Joe, she started running down the sidewalk. To have a young lady so excited to see him really boosted his ego, making him feel like a conquering hero.

Later in the evening, Dot's dad asked, "Now what, Joe?"

"Find a job," Joe answered.

"What about the GI bill? College?"

"I've got to get my high school diploma first."

"There are free classes at night for vets. You can work during the day."

"I would like to find out about that and sign up for it."

Joe started meeting Dot when she got off work and walking her home. He enjoyed having someone make a fuss over him.

When Mike got home on leave a week later, a party was arranged in the Wascura side yard Sunday after church. Several young men in the neighborhood were on leave or recently discharged, so they were the guests of honor. Joe introduced Dot to his friends and family.

Mike bought a '35 Ford for $50 and drove his parents and Joe to the appliance store where Walter and Dorotha bought an electric refrigerator and stove on credit, just a few dollars per month. A new eat-in kitchen was set up in the middle room on the main floor. They moved the cabinets and table and chairs from downstairs and installed a new sink next to the new refrigerator and stove. Joe and Mike then enclosed the side porch into a bathroom with new tub, sink and toilet. They had a plumber friend help them with the plumbing.

When he saw the toilet going in, Walter commented, "Why would anyone want to manure in his own house. That's what outhouses are for." Walter soon got used to the new convenience, but insisted that the two seat outhouse remain outback for when they were working in the garden. It was one of the last houses on Kossack St to have an indoor toilet.

The coal stove remained downstairs for heat. They got a newer used washing machine for Dorotha. It was an electric model with a wash tub with an agitator and rollers above and to the side. When finished washing you put the damp clothes through the rollers by turning the crank to get most of the water out. You then hung the clothes on the clothes lines in the backyard, which all back yards had. When it was raining or too cold to hang clothes outside, clothes were hung on clotheslines hung across a basement room or on folding dowel racks.

Beds and dressers were set up downstairs for Joe and Mike. Walter and Dorotha didn't expect them to be living there too long, as both had girlfriends.

Mike had to get back to duty as his leave was up, so Joe finished the project. After finishing, Joe found a job at a restaurant in Wilkes-Barre. He took a bus to work and decided to wait to buy a car, as he was thinking of buying rings. Many of his friends were getting engaged or married. He felt it would be nice to live in his own place with a wife to come home to.

After Christmas morning mass, Dorotha made pyrohies and cabbage and beets to go with the ham at noon. "Eat up Joe, Dorotha told him. "You are still too skinny. The Navy didn't feed you good."

"Their food wasn't as good as yours mom," Joe complimented.

Joe had been invited to Dot's home for dinner. He arrived early and asked Dot to come sit on the porch because he had a gift to give her.

"Oh, let me go get your gift," she said.

"Later, darling," Joe said nervously. "Let's sit down." He walked to the end of the porch and sat on the old medal squeaky glider. She sat next to him as he pulled a small box out of his pocket and gave it to her without saying anything, his mouth open as if looking for words.

She opened it and screamed, then hugged and kissed him. Her younger sister and dad came out to see what the screaming was about. She slipped the ring on and held out her hand for her sister to see. Now two women were screaming.

Her dad went back inside and said to his wife, "that's going to cost me. But in the long run we will save as we will have one less mouth to feed." Dot's mom knew what that meant, and ran out to the porch to her daughters.

Joe never did say anything. He was worried if he would be able to say the words, asking her to marry him, but he never had to. It was assumed, and he thought he heard a yes between screams. He never had to say anything.

While Joe's was an immigrant family who spoke a foreign language at home, Dot's family was a family that had been in the country since colonial days. Her mother was a direct descendent of the Griesemer family that had arrived in the Pennsylvania colony in 1730 from an area near Heidelberg, Germany. Another branch of her mother's family could be traced back to the original settlers of Germantown, Pennsylvania in the late 1600s. Through the years, descendants of these Germans lived throughout south central and southeast Pennsylvania. Dot's parents grew up near Harrisburg and had a family tree going back over 200 years, with all German last names. Ancestors fought in the Revolutionary war and although the first few generations were farmers, later generations were educated and professionals.

Dot's family lived in a larger house and owned a car. Not one of her relatives had ever married into an Eastern European immigrant Catholic family. Joe's parents came from a farming area where the average person went to school until they were 12. No one in Joe's family ever married a non-Catholic.

Chapter Ten

Changes

In January Dot and her sisters were busy with wedding preparations. She reserved their Lutheran church for a Saturday in late February. Her parent's home was big enough for the reception. The living room, sitting room, dining room, and porch would hold enough people. They would just have to rent some folding chairs. The cake and invitations still had to be ordered.

When Joe's parents found out Dot was not Orthodox, or Greek Catholic, or Roman Catholic, they were understanding. "She can take a class to become a Catholic so you can get married," Dorotha explained. "We can go talk to the priest."

"Well, she and her family were planning for the wedding to be at their church, the Lutheran Church," Joe informed them.

"But the Catholic Church will not recognize the marriage," Dorotha said, worried. "You will be living in sin, you will be excommunicated from the church, Joe. Your children will be conceived in sin."

"You will have to get married in our church," Walter said. "You are the man. Your wife must go to your church with you."

"I'll talk to Dot and her family," Joe said. The church was an important part of the Wascura family and the Kossack St neighborhood.

At Dot's house, Joe told her that they would have to be married at St Nicholas and the reasons why. Her parent's assumed that the wedding be held at the bride's church, since the bride's family would be paying for it. Joe didn't want his mother upset.

Dot didn't understand the non-freedom of choice insisted by the Catholic church, but she wanted to get married. As the war ended marriages were happening as fast as the GIs got home, and she didn't want to be left out. So, they sat down with Dot's parents and explained things to them.

"What the hell," her dad said loudly as he sat up in his chair, and tossed the newspaper he had been reading to the floor. "Lutherans are Christians just like the Catholics. What the hell's the difference? What's the big deal? Let me go talk to the damn priest."

"No, you won't," Dot's mom objected.

"I could see a problem if we were Jewish, or Buddhist, or Muslim, or Hindu, but a Protestant? A Christian is a Christian. It doesn't matter which denomination Christian church anyone goes to. Would it be different if we were Episcopal, Baptist, or Methodist?"

"I don't know," Joe said nervously, thinking he should rethink the whole marriage idea.

"I'm not going to pay the wedding service fee," her dad said. "If I do pay, I get to cuss out the priest. If I don't pay, then I'll keep quiet. Maybe."

"I'll pay the church fee," Joe said hoping for a compromise.

"Am I able to hold a reception for my daughter?" her dad asked sarcastically.

"The church has a hall if you wish to use it," Joe said, then wished he hadn't.

"Like hell, we'll have the reception here or at our church," her dad informed. "Are we able to attend the service?"

"Of course," Joe said cautiously.

"Catholic weddings are long," her dad pointed out. "Am I going to fall asleep?"

"I don't think so," Joe said slowly.

"I snore you know," her dad informed.

"Oh, Dad," Dot objected almost in tears.

"I do get to walk her down the aisle. Don't I?" her dad inquired.

"Of course," Joe said quietly, thinking of eloping and getting married by a justice of the peace, but the Catholic Church wouldn't recognize that ceremony either.

"Lightning won't strike the church if I walk her down the aisle, will it?" Her dad said quieter, seeing how upset the couple was. He realized they were so young. She was not yet 20 and Joe was not yet 23, but mature for his age. War will mature someone quickly.

"That's enough, you had your say," her mother said to Dot's father. Then to Joe and Dot she said, "Be sure to tell the Wascura family that they are most welcome to attend the reception at our home and we will expect them and look forward to it."

"Yes, ma'am," Joe said thankful that Dot's mom had appeared to silence her husband. Joe understood how they felt, because he felt that people looked down on Eastern Europeans. Now it was reversed with the Catholics looking down on the Protestants. He just didn't want his mother upset. Her church was so important to her.

Dot was not happy having to take the classes, but she wanted to get married, and all her friends thought Joe was so handsome and good-natured. It was obvious to her that if she didn't marry him one of her friends would snatch him up.

Mike and Andy were able to make it to the wedding in late February, but were still a few weeks from getting discharged. Walter and Dorotha were overjoyed that all their children made it to the wedding. One of Dot's brothers was unable to make it, but all her sisters did. The wedding mass was in Old Church Slavonic, which did cause Dot's father to start to fall asleep, as he didn't understand a word. Dot's mom kept her elbow busy, jabbing her husband to keep him awake.

At the reception, the two fathers toasted each other several times with whiskey shots, even after the bride and groom had left. Walter toasted the couple in Rusyn. Dot's father didn't know what he said, but lifting his glass and drank anyway. Walter's only complaint about the reception was that there was not enough room for dancing, and the choice of music.

The newlyweds took a late afternoon train to Philadelphia for their honeymoon. Then, after a couple of days there, they took the train to New York City to visit some of Joe's friends from when he had lived in there. When they got off the train in New York, they fought their way down the crowded sidewalks among the tall skyscrapers. Dot started to cry from being frightened by all the people and noise.

The next day when he wanted to take her on the ferry to the Statue of Liberty, she was afraid to go on the ferry on the choppy waters. So they just looked at the statue at a distance from the park. Any ideas Joe had about getting a higher paying job in New York, he dismissed, for he knew Dot would never want to live there.

When they got back from their short honeymoon, they moved into an apartment in Wilkes-Barre not far from their jobs. They used the buses until they were able to save for a car. One of Dot's friends married a friend of Joe's, Tom Shucosky, son of his dad's friend, Pete. Tom had been in the army occupation troops in Japan the previous October and November.

"Where in Japan were you stationed?" Joe asked him one evening when the couple was visiting Joe and Dot at their apartment.

"Hiroshima," Tom replied.

"Wasn't there a lot of radiation there," Joe asked as he and Dot served drinks.

"We were camped over 5 miles outside of the city and monitored the radiation levels constantly," Tom answered. "We stayed away from areas where there was still high radiation."

"What did they have you doing?" Joe asked.

"Our job was to keep people out of the center of the city because of the radiation. We patrolled the area for any American POW camps that might not have been found yet. We looked for any Japanese troops that hadn't been disarmed. Any Japanese officers found were to be sent to our interrogators. We had a list of Japanese officers that were on the loose, that were wanted for war crimes. But mostly, we took any Japanese who had radiation sickness and burns to the tent hospital we set up in our camp."

"How did you know if someone had radiation sickness?" Dot asked.

"There skin started to get big blisters all over parts of their bodies. It looked horrible," Tom answered.

"Did they die from the radiation sickness," Dot asked.

"Yes, many did," he replied. "We arrived two months after the blast and refugees were still wandering around untreated. We set up a refugee camp. Refugees' homes were either destroyed in the blast or burned in the firestorm after the blast. It was horrible. I will never get the images out of my mind."

"Let's hope we never have to use those type bombs again," Joe said.

"Amen," Tom said.

"To peace," Dot said holding up her cup of coffee to toast.

Walter retired in April, leaving the mine for the last time, feeling very happy that he would never be back to the dark, damp place he walked and shoveled in for so many years. No matter how poor he was, he knew he would never step in a mine again. The day after he retired, he got a letter from his youngest sister Kate that said that their father Mikel had died in January. He was 95. Kate also wrote that her father-in-law, Ian, who she knew Walter remembered, died the previous November. He had also been 95. They both were buried in the cemetery next to St Michaels.

It was not uncommon in the Carpathian Mountains to see people in their 90s tending their gardens and the animals. Always active and productive in later life, they got plenty of exercise walking around the hilly land doing chores. Their diet had plenty of vegetables and smoking was rare.

After reading the letter, Walter called his sister Annie in Chicago to tell her about their father's death. "I got a letter from Kate today, also," Annie told Walter. "I was going to call you just now to tell you about George."

"What about my brother?" Walter asked.

"He died late last night," Annie said. "He was only 63, but had been ill. That means you are the only boy left of our generation."

"And I'm not well," Walter informed her.

"I'll pray for you. Is it your lungs?"

"Yes. I feel better when I'm outside and in the garden. I retired last week."

"Good. You'll feel better not being near that coal dust. You will see. How is your family?"

"My two boys in the army just got discharged and are home now. My Navy son got out in October. He's married now."

"Bless them. They all made it home safe. Same here in Chicago. All your nephews made it home safe. God bless."

Walter told the news to Dorotha and Mike, who was staying at home. "I've got an idea, Pop," Mike said. "Andy and I are looking for jobs. But first, let's take you and mom to Chicago on the train. All it is going to cost us is the round trip train fare. We can stay at one of your sisters' homes. They all live in the same neighborhood in south Chicago. Let me call Andy."

Andy's wife was working at a factory and her mother watched their three year old. She would not be able to get off work, but thought Andy should go with them.

Walter called his sister back to tell her about the four of them coming in a few days. After taking Dorotha shopping for a couple new dresses and getting a new suit for Walter, the four of them left for Chicago a few days later.

Walter's sisters were surprised by his wavy white hair and bushy white mustache that curled up at the ends. "But at least I have hair," he said when teased about his hair turning white. "Not like your bald husbands."

"You look just like father," Annie told Walter. "The last time I saw him, his hair was turning white. You even have his big nose. You look so Rusyn."

On Sunday everyone was dressed in their Sunday best as they gathered after church for a dinner and dancing to an accordion player and Andy playing the guitar. With all the children and grandchildren of his brothers and sisters it developed into a large party with the older generation speaking in the old language. Many pictures were taken and stories of the old days told.

One day as they were taking pictures at the front steps of Annie's home, Annie waved to some neighbors walking by.

"Hello, Dimitri," she yelled.

"Hello, Annie," the man waved. "I see your relatives made it here from the east," he said speaking in Rusyn.

"Yes, this is my brother Voytek and his wife Dorotha," she answered in Rusyn.

Dimitri's eyes widened as he realized he knew her brother. "Oh my."

"Voytek, this is Dimitri and his wife Irene," Annie said.

"Call me Walter," Walter said as he shook hands with Dimitri.

215

"I think I know you," Dimitri said. "You haven't changed much except your hair and mustache are all white and you have wrinkles. We met on the ship over forty years ago."

Then Walter remembered. "The boy, Dimitri, heading to Cleveland."

"Yes. Yes."

"You grew a little taller and wider since then," Walter said as they hugged.

"Welcome to Chicago."

"Do you live here now?"

"We moved here after a few years in Cleveland to be near Irene's family."

"This calls for a toast."

Some of the Chicago relatives came to Swoyersville the next spring for Mike's wedding. After the wedding, Joe showed his brothers his new purchase, a '38 Nash, his first car, a 3 speed manual shift and four doors for only $70. Now all Walter's children owned a car. Walter said he was too old to learn to drive, and didn't plan to get one, besides he couldn't afford the gas, he told them.

Joe was also proud of the fact that Dot was pregnant with their first child, and he told everyone about it. The wedding was an opportunity for Walter and Dorotha to have their picture taken with all six children again. Now all of their children were married and the number of grandchildren was growing. After the war, the returning military got married and started having babies. The young women that had been working were now staying home to care for their babies, creating jobs for the former military, their husbands.

########

Czechoslovakia, reunited into one nation after the war, held national elections in the spring of 1946. In the election the Democratic Party won the presidency, while a communist became prime minister. In 1948 the communists started a coup, deploying police regiments and an armed workers militia. They purged the non-communists from leadership positions. Under the communists the economy became centrally planned, and private ownership of capital was abolished. The government began emphasizing the development of heavy industry.

By 1950 all church schools became state schools and all churches were put under state control. All religious newspapers and newsletters were banned. All seminaries, monasteries, and convents were closed. Private property was abolished, and cooperatives were created for agriculture. Small farm landowners received a very small percent of profits as compensation for the contribution of their land.

Kate's mother Anna had passed away in '48, just before the communists took over. They felt that it was fortunate that her parents had passed away before the communists came to power. She knew this would have upset them. Anna was laid to rest next to Mikel. They had been married 74 years when he passed away in '46.

Vasil continued to graze his livestock, and farm and hunt without much interference, as Osturna was far at the end of the road. Osturna didn't use fences, so the communist communal farming idea looked like it was in practice, whereas things continued much as they had been. The prices for farm goods was now set by the government. Since most Osturna villagers consumed most of the food they grew, they were more concerned with the price of beef and wool.

The population of Osturna was now below 1,200, but Mikolas and his new bride tried to help increase the population with a baby boy, Ivan, born in 1950. The Osturna road became paved. People installed electric wells, septic tanks, and indoor bathrooms. However, outhouses remained for outdoor convenience when working in the fields.

"I don't know how life will be for this little fellow," Vasil told Mikolas as they sat one evening in front of Vasil's house playing with Ivan. "There are so many changes with the communists. Since our farm is small, I still own it. It is still titled in our name, but they try to tell me what is to be grown and raised."

"They just took the land from the large landowners with little compensation and made them collective farms," Mikolas pointed out. "I don't think collective farms will be productive."

"Of course not. I will just keep doing what I have been doing, raising cattle and sheep, growing feed, and growing crops that we will grow for our own consumption."

"I hope the beef price holds up."

"If it doesn't than we will grow or raise whatever pays the best price."

"Little Ivan is going to have to take a bus miles to go to school when he is old enough," Mikolas complained. "They won't let the church teach the children anymore."

"I heard that too. I just hope they teach as well as the priests did."

"The election ballot next week only has communists on it, pop. What kind of choice is that? Why even go."

"I heard they would throw us in jail if we don't go vote."

Elections became a joke, as only communist party candidates were listed and only one person for each office, therefore no choice, and all officials were appointed by the communist party.

#######

Dorotha received a letter from one of her brothers in the fall of 1950 with a return address of Klenov, Czechoslovakia. At first she thought that he must have moved, but as he explained in the letter, the name of the town was changed from Klemburk to Klenov by the "Commies", as he put it. All of the fields around the village were being used for grazing of sheep and cattle, although everyone still had gardens in their back yards.

In early 1951, the cold kept Walter indoors. His cough was getting worse. Many of his old friends had either died or retired, or moved away to find a job elsewhere, as mines were closing from either no coal left, or slow demand. The population of Swoyersville had fallen below 8,000, the first census decline after almost 100 years of population increases. With the railroads all switching from steam to diesel electric locomotives, the demand for coal was falling. Power stations and steel mills were now the biggest customers for the mines. The amount of anthracite coal in northeastern Pennsylvania was becoming harder to find. With the area was running out of coal to mine, strip mining increased to get coal closer to the surface.

When the lungs can't supply enough oxygen to the heart, the heart can't get enough oxygenated blood to vital organs, which creates problems in the vital organs. For Walter, his liver stopped working properly. In addition his lungs would fill with fluid. During the spring he was in and out of the hospital. Between hospital stays he would lay in bed or on the couch, no energy to move around. After all his lifelong hard work, the pain in his chest and the difficulty to breath was hardly a reward for an honest life of providing for his family. No matter how hard he tried to breathe in through the pain, he could not get enough air in. He looked forward to weekly visits from his children and grandchildren. The neighborhood had seen so many miners dying this way, and his children knew his time would be soon.

Walter's body gave out in May and he was buried in the St Nickolas Church Cemetery on the hill at the end of Kossack St., next to Walter Jr. He had fourteen grandchildren with three more on the way.

After the funeral, the children worried about Dorotha. The house was paid for, but the only income she had was a meager miner pension widow benefit and a small social security widow benefit.

"Don't worry about me," Dorotha told her children. "I'll be dead myself soon. I'm turning 71 soon. I have my vegetable garden and chickens. I won't starve. I'll stay here."

None of the children had room in their homes for their mother. But they knew she wouldn't be able to afford to keep the house in good condition with her meager income. Shortly after the funeral, Joe found out that the restaurant he was working at in a coal mine town east of Wilkes-Barre, was closing. The mines near the town closed and with local businesses closing, the restaurant's business declined to the point it was losing money. Joe was able to get a job at a restaurant in Wilkes-Barre, but it was too far to drive from where they lived.

"You are welcome to move in here," Dorotha told Joe. "You live in the upstairs rooms and I'll stay downstairs. The coal stove is still there and it still works. In the winter it heats those rooms."

"I'll only be here for a while until I get some money saved for a place of our own," Joe promised.

"Or you can add on to this house," Dorotha suggested. "Like your father had always planned." It had been so long since little children had lived in the house, she looked forward to being busy. The emptiness she felt since Walter passed away would be gone with the sounds of two little boys.

Joe put in new linoleum floors in the bathroom and upstairs kitchen, and wall-papered rooms. Joe's two sons would be in the small upstairs bedroom, while he and Dot would be in the larger upstairs bedroom with a crib for the baby that was due any day. Downstairs Joe put a new linoleum floor in the kitchen and in what became Dorotha's bedroom. Dorotha's loom was positioned under the stairs.

Soon after moving in, the two little boys were calling Dorotha "Grandma Downstairs". Dot had a baby girl at a nearby hospital shortly after they moved in. Grandma

Downstairs made pyrohies for the boys often, to their delight, and she showed Dot how to make them.

Dorotha and Joe always spoke a combination of Rusyn, Slovak, and English to each other as was the custom of the family. But it was always just English when Dot or the boys were part of the conversation. When Dorotha didn't know the English word she would just use the old language and Joe would translate.

The boys loved to play in the garden and help grandma. Dorotha would swing them in the "Grandma swing" as the boys called it. She would tell them that Grandpa had made the swing with the help of a neighbor and their uncle Jake, who was their age when he helped his dad.

In 1954 Dorotha bought a used TV from a store. Joe put an antenna on the roof and the nightly ritual was to go downstairs to the couch in the downstairs kitchen and watch TV before bedtime. Roy Rogers, the Lone Ranger, Gene Autry, I Love Lucy, and others were the boys' favorites. For Christmas they asked Santa Claus for a Roy Rogers hat and playset. Grandma Downstairs always had homemade cookies and milk waiting for the children's TV time.

The next year prices were dropping on TVs, although still expensive for the average consumer. Stores would offer them for credit at a few dollars per month. Joe and Dot bought one for their upstairs living room, making their house the first house on Kossack St to have two TVs. On weekday mornings that there was no school, the boys would watch Captain Kangaroo. After school they would catch the Mickey Mouse Club on TV.

While at the old Wascura house Joe paid the utilities and taxes and insurance on the house. They saved money for when they could get a bigger house. When their daughter was over four years old and still in a crib in her parent's bedroom, Joe knew it was time to move on.

They found a three bedroom duplex to rent for $25 per month on the hill of a neighboring town. He offered for Dorotha to come move with them and sell her house, but she wanted to keep her house and garden. Now she would have the house to herself. Dorotha now felt too old to have little ones under foot. She often escaped to the garden to get some peace and quiet. Now she could just go to the garden when she felt like it, and rest on her grandma swing when she got tired.

She only had a few chickens left for eggs and the pigs had been gone since before Walter died. For the first time in her life she would be living alone, but all of her fellow neighborhood widows would make sure she got a ride to church or the store as needed.

"I will expect one of my children to be here each Sunday after church with their family," Dorotha told her children. "I will cook, so come hungry. Plus a grandchild can come spend time here and stay over when school is out for vacation."

Like Dorotha, several elderly miners' widows lived on Kossack St. They all attended St Nickolas and helped each other get around, even though none of them had a car or knew how to drive. The church would make sure someone would get them to church events, which was just a mile away.

Houses rented for less on the steep hill of the town Joe moved to. When it snowed people couldn't get their cars up the hill and would have to park them several blocks away. However, the kids loved living on the hill in winter and would wish for plenty of snow. The kids would start at their front yard with their sleds and sled down the side yard, then all the way to the end of the back yard, increasing speed as they went. Going to school in the snow was easy as the kids just slid down the hill on their boots. However, going home was more challenging.

After moving to their rental, Dot started taking their daughter to the Lutheran Church in town, while Joe took the boys to the Byzantine Ruthenian Church in the town. The church services were in Old Church Slavonic, so the young boys did not understand what was being said. The boys felt that the Catholic Church service was designed to keep boys awake. Between the moving from sitting to standing to kneeling on the knee pads, and singing, a boy could not take a nap. Occasionally Joe would take the boys to a Roman Catholic Church where part of the service was in English. This way Joe felt they could understand part of the service, even though they wouldn't understand the Latin part.

Dot discouraged her children from learning the "old language". "It will slow them up in school," she would say. She didn't want Joe or Dorotha teaching them the old language.

Now that the children were no longer living above Grandma Downstairs, they were no longer hearing the Slovak or Rusyn words spoken between their father and grandmother. So, any words previously learned were now being forgotten as they grew.

In 1958 Joe and Dot had another daughter. When the baby was a month old, Dot had her one sister and her husband come by the house on Sunday and take her and the baby to the Lutheran Church to have the baby baptized. The three older children had been baptized in the Catholic Church.

When Dot and Joe argued about it later, Dot told him, "It doesn't matter where the baby was baptized, as long as it's a Christian church. At least they speak English at the Lutheran Church. You take the boys to the Catholic Church like you have been doing. Drop me and the girls off at the Lutheran Church each week on your way."

"The family should all go together to the man's church," Joe argued.

"That's not going to happen," Dot demanded.

To keep peace in the home, Joe dropped Dot and the girls off at the Lutheran Church before taking the boys with him to the Catholic Church each Sunday.

On the 1960 Presidential Election Joe voted for John Kennedy. He liked that Kennedy was a war hero who had fought in the Navy in the Pacific like he had, and was also a Catholic. Joe felt that Kennedy would be less likely to be influenced by campaign contributions because Kennedy had his own money. Dot voted for Nixon, who was non-Catholic.

Chapter Eleven

Opportunities

Joe had a special recipe he had developed for a batter for breaded fish fillets at the restaurant he worked at. He would soak the fillets in the batter, then place them in the first breading mix, then to a second batter, and finally in another breading. The fillets would be placed in a shallow fryer of special oils for a specified time.

Lines would form at the front of the buffet restaurant before 11 am every Friday. Being a Catholic area, people ate no red meat on Fridays. During Lent, they would be busy almost every day. The Times Leader newspaper even wrote a story with pictures of the long lines.

In early 1964, Joe went to the owner to ask for a raise. He was making $88 per week. For his salary he worked five nine hour days and one five hour day. His rent was now $45 per month. The owner of the restaurant also had a large grocery store, butcher supply business, and bakery next store to the restaurant.

"Joe, my overall business right now is down over last year," the old owner explained to Joe. "With all the anthracite mines closing and the strip mines slowing down, people are moving away and I have less customers. True, the restaurant is doing better, but the other businesses are not. I just can't give a raise right now. Maybe later in the year."

Joe had two boys in high school that he wanted to go to college, but he knew he couldn't help them with expenses. They would have to have good summer jobs and part time jobs to work their way through. But where would they get a job? For years, Joe would reupholster furniture for people to help earn money. He would come home at night and work on people's furniture. The boys would pull tacks from the furniture to remove the old fabric, which would be used as a pattern for Dot to cut the new fabric. Dot would do any sewing and then Joe would tack the new fabric and batting on to the furniture piece. Sometimes Joe would also do landscaping work for people. The family always had a spring vegetable garden in the backyard to help with expenses. Joe was always working, sun up to sun down.

Shortly after Joe's talk with his boss, Dot got a call from her brother in Chicago. He had just bought a fried chicken franchise and was quitting his management job at Kraft Foods. He was interviewing management staff to run the place as the restaurant was being built. He would manage it at first, then let the staff operate it, as he moved on to open another restaurant. Fast food restaurants were new. It had been only a few years since the first McDonalds had opened.

Dot told her brother about Joe being turned down for a raise. "The business is not good around here right now," Dot told him. "People are getting laid off."

"You need to consider moving to Chicago," he suggested.

"Why would we move all the way out there?" she asked.

"Because Chicago is growing. Business is booming. Wages are higher. Joe can make 30 or 40 percent more here. Remember, I hire people for Kraft. I know the market. He would have to come out here on vacation first and apply for jobs. Pennsylvania is declining. You got to get your kids out of there. No jobs for them there."

"That's something to think about," Dot agreed.

"I'll ask around and think of places for him to apply."

After hanging up, it occurred to her brother that he should consider interviewing Joe for his new business. Joe had been in the restaurant business for years. A week later her brother called back and asked to talk to Joe. "How would you like to be an assistant manager at my restaurant, Joe? I'd start you at $125 per week. I've sent you information on the restaurant. It should arrive in a couple of days. Don't give me an answer until you look over the information. I'll need your answer in a week. There are plenty of colleges in the Chicago area, and plenty of places for the boys to work during summers and weekends during school. I know how important it is to you to have your children go to college."

Joe thanked him, and said he would call him back in a week. When the information arrived he studied it and decided he could not turn down a 42 percent raise in income. But he had no money to pay for a moving company.

Joe sat on his front porch as he reviewed the information from Dot's brother. The spring winds came from the mountains, bringing the pleasing smell of melting snow, evergreen trees, and early flowers, refreshing the air like a promise of better life ahead.

When Joe called his brother-in-law back, they worked out a deal where Joe would come out now and stay with him or one of Joe's cousins. Joe would save money for a rental home, and Dot's brother would pay for the moving company. The family would move after school was out. It was settled and Joe and Dot became part of the American population shift of the 1960s, east to west and cities to suburbs.

"I'm frightened about this move," Dot told Joe the night before Joe was to leave for Chicago. He would be driving their '55 fading green Plymouth sedan half way across the country. It would be over a 15 hour drive as the interstates were not complete all the way. He planned to sleep in the back seat after driving about ten hours.

"Don't worry, it will be fine," Joe assured her as he packed his suitcase. "I'll be making more money and that will be good."

"It's so far and such a big city. I don't like big cities."

"I'll be working outside the city and we'll be living outside the city."

"Find us a house to rent, definitely not an apartment."

"I'll keep you informed as I look, dear."

"It's going to be three months without you. You be careful driving. I made sandwiches for you to eat on the way. They're in the refrigerator. I'll make a thermos of hot coffee for you in the morning. I put a blanket and pillow in the back seat for when you stop to sleep."

Despite appearing brave, Joe was nervous about going. But everyone he had talked to encouraged him to go for it. The day before he left, a sinkhole opened up on a road in their town. It swallowed up a big section of the road and a man's front yard and front porch. The old mines would fill with water and when the water receded, the mine would collapse, causing the sinkhole at the surface. "I guess that's a sign that it is time to leave," Joe told his children. One time, a sinkhole had opened under the river, causing the river to flow into the mines. Many railroad cars were dumped into the river to plug the sinkhole.

Chicago was growing fast into the suburbs, which caused a shortage of housing and rent increases. The restaurant was being built in a western suburb. Joe had a shock when trying to rent a house. The least expensive he could find was a three bedroom townhouse for $140 per month, $95 more than what they were paying in Pennsylvania. In northeastern Pennsylvania, with population leaving, there were more than enough old houses for rent, therefore low rents. In Chicago, with a growing population, houses and apartments would be rented as fast as they could be built.

Despite the increase in expense, Joe financially benefited. Within a two and a half years, Joe was making three times his previous Pennsylvania weekly salary, managing a burger restaurant, after Dot's brother sold his chicken restaurant. Joe heard from friends in Pennsylvania that told him that the restaurant he had worked at no longer had the long lines on Friday. Joe called his former manager to say he was sorry that their business was down, and let it be known about his latest raises and bonuses.

#######

In 1968 a reform movement started in Czechoslovakia to try to democratize socialism. Social democrats began to form a separate party. The reform movement wanted to improve relations with all countries regardless of their social systems. The movement wanted guaranteed freedom of religion, press, assembly, speech, and travel. The internal reforms and foreign policy statements of the new leadership created great concern for the Soviets. As a result, the Soviet troops invaded Czechoslovakia. Popular opposition was expressed in numerous spontaneous acts of nonviolent resistance. In Prague and other cities throughout the country, Czechs and Slovaks greeted Soviet soldiers with arguments and reproaches.

Mikolas' son, Ivan, and some of his friends took a train to Bratislava to protest near where the Soviet troops parked their trucks and tanks on the street. Ivan, 18, had just graduated from high school two months earlier, and had been accepted to the University of Economics in Bratislava. He was scheduled to start school, so he went a couple of days earlier with his friends to Bratislava to protest. They would yell "go home" to the soldiers along with insults. They knew not to throw anything at a soldier for fear of being fired at.

Ivan called his parents after he was on campus a couple of days, as he had been instructed by his parents. "Are you all settled in?" Mikolas asked him.

"Yes. Food is not that great though."

"You are there to study, not get fat. Besides no one can cook as good as your mom and grandma. You're not out in the streets with those other protesters are you?"

"Why not?" Ivan realized after he said it, that it was not wise to ask the question.

"You'll get arrested. You're there to study."

"You're right. But you see the troops are next to campus. You can't help but see them when you go to class. So we all say nasty things to them as we walk by."

"Just move fast when you go through campus."

"I do."

The Czechoslovakia leadership declared that the invasion was a violation of socialist principles, international laws, and UN charter. But the outcome resulted in communist party control of the media, and suppression of the Czechoslovakia Social Democratic Party. There would be no reform, and the Soviet Union thereafter paid more attention to any reform attempts. The frustration of a planned economy continued. Waiting in lines for simple items continued. Being put on lists to take your turn to buy large items like appliances, also continued.

Vasil and Kate would get letters from Kate's sisters in America telling of the newest appliance they got, or of the newest stores, or of their latest car, or of all the TV channels they received with their new latest antenna. Vasil and Kate wanted to go to America for a vacation to visit relatives, but travel restrictions increased after the protests and they were not able to. Kate's relatives were afraid to travel to a communist country for a vacation, especially after seeing the TV news of Soviet troops in the streets of Bratislava and Prague.

#######

Joe's oldest sister, Ann, and her husband had retired in the late 60s and moved from Philadelphia to Dorotha's house to take care of her. Dorotha was in her late 80s and still gardening. For years one of her grandchildren would come to her house for a few weeks each summer. In June 1972, one of her grandsons, Marko, was staying in the bottom floor for the summer. He was a student at Wilkes College. During summers he would stay at the Wascura house as he had a summer job nearby.

Kossack St had always been prone to flooding after heavy rains. The Wascura house was on the flat part of Kossack St, two miles from the river. The house was a block from the hill. In 1936 the flood of the Susquehanna River caused the house to flood the bottom floor. The flood was a foot below the front door, about four feet above the ground. People in boats would come to bring them food for several days. It took a week for the river to subside. Then the town brought pumps

236

to pump out basements. Their kitchen, which was downstairs at the time, was ruined and Walter had to redo it. After the flood the state built dykes along the river.

Although hurricanes rarely ever arrive in northeastern Pennsylvania, occasionally the rains of one will affect the mountains as it weakens over land. Hurricane Agnes moved up the east coast in June 1972. It slowed as the west part of the storm dumped rain on northeastern Pennsylvania. As the storm stalled, it unloaded all its moisture for three days, June 21st to the 23rd, eighteen inches in total. The Susquehanna River, already filled with melted snow and spring rains, started to reach the tops of the dikes. Marko volunteered with some friends at the Forty Fort dike by putting sand bags on the top to make the dikes higher. On the 23rd, as they placed bags, the river was going over the top of the bags as fast as they could place them.

Marko was soaked from the rain despite his parka and boots, as water flowed ankle deep over the bags. The National Guard arrived and ordered everyone to evacuate the area. As the volunteers headed to their cars near the Forty Fort cemetery, a noise of moving earth caused Marko to look back at the dike. A section of the dike by the cemetery had broken apart causing a rush of river water to head toward them, bringing earth with it.

Marko jumped into his car, hoping to get far enough down the road before the water got too high and stalled his engine. As he looked in his rearview mirror he could see a casket floating down the street, pulled up by the raging river.

He headed due west to the Wascura house to get his almost 91 year old grandmother, 70 year old uncle, and 63 year old aunt. He drove 50 mph down the 30 speed limit streets. Railroad tracks separated Forty Fort and Swoyersville and the rail bed stood three foot above the road. He made it there before the waters could stall his car, giving him time as the water was only a foot on the other side of the rail bed. But in short time the river would be raging over the rail bed, so he had to hurry. He blew his horn as he approached the house.

He ran into the house yelling, "The dike broke we've got to get out of here."

"We'll be OK," Dorotha said. "Just move your bed and clothes up here, in case the downstairs floods."

"No, quick, the water will be up to where you are sitting now," he yelled. "We won't be able to get out of here without a boat in about 15 minutes. I'll drive us to Uncle Andy's." Andy lived 25 miles north, but on the other side of the river.

When he finally got them out of the house, they had to wade through a foot of water. He and his uncle helped Dorotha through the water to the car. He had left the car running. The water was almost covering the tailpipe. His uncle's car needed a new carburetor, so they knew it wouldn't start, so they had to leave it.

Marko was relieved when he got to the hill. He stopped at the corner of Main St and Kossack St to look down the hill. The water was already up to the porch of the house. He drove north hoping to find a pay phone working and not in use. He didn't know how far he would have to drive to find a bridge open. Traffic was congested and moving at less than 20 mph with everyone on the high roads trying to escape the flood.

Finally after an hour he was able to find a working phone without a long line and reached Andy, who had been calling Dorotha's house. Andy told him he would meet him further north in Tunkhannock to see if that bridge was open.

When they got there the river was almost up to the bridge. Police were only letting one car go across at a time, so the backup was a mile long. As night fell, they got across, and Andy was waiting on the other side. By the time they got to Andy's house, Marko had driven over fifty miles to get there.

A few days later Andy, one of his sons, and Marko drove to Main St and Kossack St to see if the river was receding. With binoculars they could see that the water was half way up the main floor, about eight foot above the ground. Water marks on the siding showed that it had receded about a foot from its high water mark. The house also looked like it was leaning slightly.

"The stone foundation must be giving way," Andy commented. "All their furniture is ruined. Some clothing might be able to be saved after washing several times. But some may still smell."

Realizing that the house was going to be unlivable for a while, if at all, Andy found two one bedroom apartments across the hall from each other at a new senior housing building only a few blocks from his home. They would just have to pay a percentage of their social security as rent. Andy called friends and relatives for donations of furniture and clothing. Dorotha's other children and grandchildren sent money and clothing.

Two weeks after the flood, Dorotha walked into her new apartment and saw it set up with new furniture, dishes, pots and pans, and new clothing hanging in the closet. "I hope we didn't forget anything," Andy said to Dorotha as she cried with joy.

"I have been blessed," Dorotha said as she hugged everyone gathered there. She was proud her apartment, as she showed off her new furniture to visitors. Children, grandchildren, and great-grandchildren came bringing gifts. Ann, who was just across the hall, and Dorotha cooked and ate their meals together.

Three weeks after the start of the flood people were allowed back to their homes to get belongings. The river had receded back to its banks but the county and state inspectors still had to determine if each house was livable and could be occupied. Andy and other family members took a gas pump to pump out the downstairs. They gathered what they could salvage. They brought a van with them for any wooden furniture they thought might be repairable. The foundation was collapsed and the house had a slight lean to it.

They carefully walked through the house gathering clothing in hopes that it would come clean and not smell after washing. Dorotha's 1902 wedding photo, which had sat on a table for years, and had recently been put on the wall because the back of the frame had broken, had escaped damage. The high water mark was just below the photo.

When most of the water was out of the downstairs, the foundation started to crumble more, and the house leaned another foot. Marko ran downstairs in his boots and started passing stuff out of the downstairs.

After the vehicles were filled they stood around talking about coming back the next day with wood to prop the house up, when two county inspectors drove up. They had come to walk in the house to look for structural damage. As they came out of the house after their inspection, the house leaned of few more inches.

"There is too much damage to the supporting beams," the one inspector said. "It is not salvageable. In another day it will be completely collapsed. You will have to rebuild from the ground up."

"Or sell the piece of land," Andy said with tears in his eyes. "Forget about coming back with wood, boys." Andy and the other children had been born and raised in the house. It was the only home for Dorotha for over 50 years. The inspectors nailed a condemned notice on the front of the house before they left. The inspectors said that the state would be bull dozing it in a few weeks and hauling it away.

On the way back to Andy's house they heard on the radio that an estimated 2,000 caskets had been uprooted during the flood from the Forty Fort Cemetery and other cemeteries in the area. Some caskets were over two hundred years old. The caskets and skeletons were placed in a mass grave on a hill where the river could not disturb them again.

When they got back, they took the wedding photo to Dorotha and hung it on the wall of her apartment. She cried and hugged everyone for saving it. It showed a slender young smiling bride of a time so long ago. The portly 91 year old white haired grandmother still had the same smile.

One day the next week, Dorotha was rocking in her chair watching her new TV when a knock came at the door. She slowly walked to the door with her cane. She yelled "Joe" as she opened the door and saw her smiling son with his wife and two daughters, who had traveled a long way to see her. After much excited hugs and kisses she showed him around the apartment and the old pictures that had been saved. It was a chance for Joe to use the old language with his mom.

"It is God's will that I have this nice place," she told Joe in the old language. "The old house had served its purpose, a home to raise our children, to live our lives as a family. This is better for me, and with Ann across the hall to share meals with." No matter how little she had, Dorotha was always happy

242

and pleased with whatever she had, and always optimistic about the future.

Ann and Joe cooked a big dinner for their mother as relatives came and went out of the two apartments, where the doors remained open all day. As she had aged Dorotha spoke more in the language of her youth, forgetting English words. But she never lost her smile or sense of humor.

Dorotha lived past her 92nd birthday. She was buried next to Walter and Walter Jr. on the hill overlooking Kossack St, where the family had been born, grew up, and lived for so many years. She had taught her daughters, daughter-in-laws, and granddaughters how to make pyrohies and other dishes from the old country. She had 19 grandchildren.

Chapter Twelve

Democracy

In the early 70s Joe and Dot moved south to Georgia, becoming part of the new US population shift to the south. Eventually, Joe bought a small restaurant in the downtown area of the town and a home on the outskirts.

One evening in 1984, Joe felt chest pains as he sat in his recliner after a long day. After getting home from work that day, Joe had chopped some wood for the fireplace that he had built from bricks from the old courthouse that he got for free. With the chest pains not going away, Dot got worried and called a neighbor to come over. Joe said it was probably just bad indigestion. Dot asked the neighbor to drive them to the hospital. "It won't hurt to get checked out," Dot persuaded him.

At the hospital the doctor said it was a heart attack and admitted him. The next day he had another heart attack while lying in the hospital bed. Joe asked for a priest. The town had just one Roman Catholic Church and that priest came. When someone was possibly dying, the Roman Catholic priest gives last rites, which are the sacraments of anointing of the sick, penance, and the Eucharist. But Joe, being familiar with the byzantine-rite church, which did not follow the Latin liturgies, wanted the sacred sacraments and prayers of the Eastern Byzantine church, which would include reception of Holy Communion. The priest told him he did not know these particular prayers, and certainly not in Slavonic. A nurse offered to find an Orthodox priest for him. The nearest byzantine-rite eastern Orthodox or Greek Catholic Church was over an hour's drive away, and a priest agreed to come to do the sacred sacraments of Confession and Holy Communion.

After Joe's third heart attack in as many days, the cardiologist told one of Joe's sons that a bypass was the only thing that would save him. But he would have to be taken by ambulance over an hour away to the nearest hospital that was equipped to do bypasses. The son had to pay for the ambulance before the ambulance would transport him to the other hospital, as Joe had no medical insurance.

The operation was a success, and Joe felt better, but weak after the operation. The day after the operation, the nurse made him cough up fluid building up in his lungs. When he coughed, the fluid he spat up was brown. "Why is it brown," Joe asked the nurse.

"Because you are a smoker," she answered him.

"But I haven't smoked in over five years," Joe pointed out.

"Where did you think that tobacco smoke clogging your lungs was going to go?" she asked. "It's covering the inside of your lungs making it hard for your blood to get refreshed with oxygen, and making your heart work harder."

When home from the hospital, Joe's children took turns visiting, and taking Joe on slow walks. They helped with exercises that the doctor told him to do, to help the healing of the bones and muscles that were cut in the surgery. The walking was hard on his one leg, where a vein was taken out and used in the bypass.

After recovery, and once back to work only a month after the heart attack, Joe began to make plans to retire in four or five years after he turned 65. He planned to sell the restaurant and travel to visit their children who lived in different states.

One evening as Joe and Dot strolled along their street, as advised by his doctor, Joe told Dot, "I'm glad none of the children ever smoked like you and I. I'd hate to see one of them have to go through an operation like I had to."

"I hope I stopped smoking in time," Dot said. "I would hate to have that same operation. Not to mention we can't afford it."

"That's for sure. We need to save our money for retiring and going to Florida in the winter. We can do that as soon as I pay for this operation. We can start saving, and in about five years, sell the restaurant and retire." Joe still had the ability to look forward, and turn a situation into a positive.

Joe's brother Mike died in the spring of '87 of lung cancer. Mike had been a lifelong smoker like Joe. Their sister Mary had died ten years earlier. Joe's other three siblings were retired. In the summer of '87, Andy's sons organized a family reunion at the home of one of Andy's sons in northeastern Pennsylvania. They would also be celebrating Jake's 75th birthday.

Joe's four children flew with him to northeastern Pennsylvania for the reunion. Joe's gray hair and mustache were starting to turn white, which got many comments about how much he looked like Walter. Joe's bushy mustache that curled at the ends was a mix of gray and white just like Walter's. A polka record was brought out so Joe could polka with the ladies.

During the reunion, they calculated that all 19 grandchildren had graduated from high school and nine had college degrees, four of which were Joe's four children, something he was most proud of. The family's history was like the history of many immigrant families, where the turn of the century immigrants came for a better life, and passed that dream on to their children and grandchildren.

#######

Throughout '88 and '89, anti-Communist demonstrations took place in Bratislava, Prague, and other cities in Czechoslovakia. In November of '89, the communist police violently broke up a peaceful pro-democracy demonstration, and had brutally beaten many student participants. Several groups had united and formed the Civic Forum, protesting for bureaucratic reform and civil liberties.

By November 20th protesters in Prague grew to 500,000, protesting the one party government. It quickly gained the support of millions of Czech and Slovaks, being referred to as the Velvet Revolution, which resulted in communist party leaders resigning and officials electing a non-communist president in December. The Soviets did not interfere, as their economy was in decline, and they couldn't afford their large army anymore. The Soviets had decided that each country in Eastern Europe should be free to deal with reform as it pleased.

A coalition government, in which the communists had a minority of positions, was formed that month, and a free election was scheduled for June '90. Over ninety percent of the population voted in the election, and as anticipated, the non-communists won landslide victories in local governments and a majority in the federal parliament.

But Slovaks wanted greater autonomy. As a result, in July '92 leaders of Czechoslovakia worked out an agreement that the Czech area and the Slovak area would become separate republics. On January 1, 1993, the Czech Republic and Slovakia were peacefully founded.

Ivan, who had been elected mayor of Osturna, had the church bells rung at one second after midnight, on the start of January 1st. Town mayor was an unpaid office and leader of the town council, which were also unpaid. The council met once a month.

As the bells tolled Ivan stood with his arms around his wife and their twelve year old son, Simon, in front of the town hall with many of the town residents, now less than 1,000. A celebration was planned, despite the late hour.

After the bells tolled, the music started and the young ones danced. A bonfire lit up the night. Wine and brandy were passed out for many toasts. Ivan made a speech, saying that he felt this was going to be good for Slovakia and Osturna. His dad Mikolas, now 72, hugged his son and many other residents. Mikolas had been on the town council in the past as had his father, Vasil, who passed away seven years earlier at the age of 96. Kate had died a year later.

"I wish my parents were here to see this day," Mikolas told Ivan. "It would make them so happy. My father always used to talk about the democracy days from 1919 to 1939."

"Simon, you remember this day," Ivan told his son. "Now it is up to us to make sure it works." Just then their wives grabbed them for a dance.

The Osturna area was mostly pasture for beef cattle, dairy cows, and sheep. With the Tatra Mountain National Park next to Osturna, Ivan was hoping to build a small hotel for hikers and mountain bikers in the summer and skiers in the winter. With the communists gone he was more hopeful of doing this. He felt investors would be easier to find now. He owned a couple of 100 year old houses that he furnished and rented out to hikers and skiers. The houses had been added to and remodeled over the years, so they weren't quite the same as 100 years earlier.

A unicameral legislature of 150 representatives was set up, parliamentary style, with a president and a prime minister. Slovakia, which had been 85 percent agriculture in 1900 now had just over ten percent agriculture. Slovakia was still forty percent forested, but much of the forests were in the high Tatras and other mountains of the Carpathian range. The lumber industry was not that large, and Slovaks had always had a respect for the forests. In Osturna, it had been a practice for generations that if you cut one, plant one.

Ivan worked in a nearby town, but lived in Osturna. His children went to school in the town where he worked, as these were the closest schools. He would often drive the children to school, but if he was going to be out of town on business, the children would just take the school bus. With the fall of communism, the state was selling off property and buildings to raise capital. Ivan and several other friends were hoping to get a bank loan or buy on payments from the government. They planned to keep their jobs and invest in their spare time. They felt now was the time to go into debt for a brighter future, and Ivan felt the prices would not be low for long.

One evening the following summer, as Ivan and his friends sat behind Ivan's house calculating estimates of finances, the wind from the mountains brought the pleasing smell of trees and flowers, refreshing the air like a promise of better life ahead. "I'm glad those mountains were made a National Park," he commented.

########

Before Joe's heart attack he had hired a new cook at his restaurant. The cook was a Mexican who had worked at a textile mill in a nearby town, but had cooking experience. The mill had had a layoff, and with a wife and three young toddlers, he took whatever job he could find. When Joe went into the hospital, Jose, the cook, helped the head waitress run the restaurant while Joe was gone. Joe paid them each a bonus during the month he was out.

Jose and his wife were renting an old small house in a neighborhood lined with narrow houses on unpaved streets. The old houses were in need of painting and repair, and were only twenty feet wide, with only ten feet between each house. Grass and weeds were few as dirt was the main landscaping. The entire neighborhood was owned by one old landlord that had inherited it from his grandfather. The small back yards were filled with clotheslines, and some front yards were filled with old junk cars that didn't run. The houses rented by the week for between $40 and $50. Not a bargain the 1984, but less then nearby apartments or larger houses, that required the rent to be paid monthly.

A few weeks after Joe returned to work, he and Dot had decided not to buy Christmas gifts for each other in order to save some money. His children had used up vacation time visiting Joe during his hospital stay and after, so no one would be visiting during Christmas.

The restaurant would be closed on Christmas day, and since Christmas Eve fell on a Sunday that year, it would be closed on Christmas Eve, since the restaurant was always closed on Sundays. On Saturday, the 23rd, Joe was helping Jose clean up late in the afternoon, and asked Jose about what he got his little children for Christmas.

"We didn't get them anything except clothes," Jose explained. "We will just wrap the clothes and give them the gifts in the morning. They will be happy to open anything."

"I'm sure they will be happy to see gifts under the tree on Christmas morning," Joe said.

"We don't have a tree," Jose admitted. "We had to send money to my mom in Mexico. She is not well."

"I'm sorry to hear that. I hope she is feeling better."

When Joe got home that evening, he told Dot about his conversation with Jose and then after church on Sunday morning, Joe talked to Dot about charity. "We should be thankful for what we do have, instead of our bad luck lately. Let's buy some inexpensive toys and a small tree, and take it to Jose's home tonight."

Dot smiled. "What ages are they?"

"One, three and four. Boy, girl, boy."

"Let's go find something."

They enjoyed shopping for inexpensive toys; blocks and a little truck for the one year old boy, a small doll and a dress for the three year old girl, and a fire engine and a ball for the four year old boy. They bought a boxed three foot decorated Christmas tree, and a Santa hat for Joe. Dot wrapped the Christmas presents at home, and wrapped a nut roll desert she had made in aluminum foil. Joe's mom had taught her how to make the desert years before.

Late in the afternoon, Joe and Dot drove to Jose's home. When they got there, Joe put on the Santa hat and took the tree out of the box and carefully carried the tree to the door. Dot carried the wrapped presents, as Joe yelled "Ho, Ho, Ho, Merry Christmas", several times. Jose opened the door with his four year old standing behind him with wide eyes looking at the tree and presents.

The children happily posed and smiled for Dot, as she took pictures of the children opening gifts. Jose's wife cut the nut roll into pieces for everyone, as the four year old sang "feliz navida" for everyone. The home was sparsely furnished with well-worn furniture. It reminded Joe and Dot of when they were first married and made them feel thankful this season.

Chapter Thirteen

Retirement

Joe was watching a TV news segment of the Slovakian independence that New Year's day in '93, when he decided to call his brother Andy. "Andy, do you think the villages of mom and pop are in Slovakia?" Joe asked him after telling Andy about what he saw on the news.

"It's possible, but the boundaries in Eastern Europe have changed so much in the last 90 years," Andy said. "Who knows?"

"Well the villages were in eastern Czechoslovakia, when it was created," Joe pointed out. "So I'm assuming that they are in Slovakia now, being Slovakia was in the east half of Czechoslovakia."

"I agree. How's retirement?"

"Fine. I work mornings at a convenience store three blocks from the house," Joe said. "It helps pay the bills."

"I work part time too. I work for my son half of each day. You know, he's a contractor and is always needing supplies, so I drive his pickup to get what he needs. It saves him time. He pays me cash each week. Like you say, it helps pay the bills."

"Sometimes the store wants me to work more than four hours," Joe complained. "But I can't stand to be on this one leg for too long. You know the one they took a vein out of to use on my bypass."

"I know what you mean," Andy sympathized. "Since my heart attack, I've learned not to lift anything heavy. The lumberyard loads for me, and my son's workers unload. I don't want to have one of those bypasses."

Joe had sold the restaurant three years earlier, but a year later Dot had a cancer operation that used up most of the profit of selling the restaurant. Back in the '70s, when he bought the restaurant, he could not find a health insurance company to cover Dot because of a preexisting heart condition. He could get insurance on Dot that would cover other problems, but not heart related problems. Since he had never had health issues himself, he decided to get little health insurance on either of them. Joe realized his mistake when he had to have bypass surgery. He paid the last of that bill before he sold the restaurant. Now he needed to work part time to supplement his social security.

A year before he sold the restaurant, one of Joe's regular customers, Ralph, a reporter for the local newspaper, wrote a poem about Joe and the restaurant. Ralph had always ordered the same breakfast every day. He would just say "good morning, Joe," and sit down.

"Good morning to you, Ralph," Joe would reply in a loud voice and Ralph's breakfast would be prepared. Mornings were always very busy at the restaurant. Whenever a regular left each day, Joe would yell "Have a nice day," and the person's name if he knew it.

One morning Ralph handed Joe the morning newspaper. "When you get a chance Joe read this," Ralph said pointing to a poem in the paper. A few minutes later Joe sat down with a cup of coffee and was surprised to see a poem titled "Joe's Grill".

There's a grill up the street

Where each morning friends meet

For coffee and a word or two.

They come in with a howdy,

Hey Joe! Give me my regular please.

People sit and chat, two or three to a booth

Everybody always in their place.

But if someone enters a strange face

They're quickly made to feel at home.

Hey waitress! Coffee please.

There's a table up front that seats eight or ten

Where the same singles usually gather

To hear the same warm patter.

Some folks are greeters, yet some stay alone

Their head in the paper, their thoughts their own.

They come and go at their set times

Moving on slowly into life each day,

Ya'll have a good one, you hear!

As you go out the door you might hear Joe cry

Hey! I need some water up here!

The same words and faces help start each day

For outside that door, to face the fray.

And it's nice to have friends that say

Hey Ralph, have a nice day!

"This is good," Joe said laughing. "I got to make copies of this."

"I thought you would say that, so I made copies for you," Ralph said handing him copies. "Here you can show it to your customers."

Joe got up and yelled in his deep loud voice, "Everybody, Ralph wrote about the grill in the newspaper today. Everybody buy a copy of the newspaper and I'll autograph it," he said jokingly. "Your breakfast is on the house today, Ralph. I'll have to mail copies to my children."

In retirement, Joe took a nap after getting home each day from the convenience store, then he would work in his vegetable garden. When he had the restaurant, he would often use some vegetables from his garden at the restaurant. "Those came from my garden," he would proudly tell his customers.

His afternoon nap on his recliner would relieve the angina pain he felt after working for four or five hours standing at the register at the convenience store. After a couple hours in his recliner, he felt better and would work in the yard if cool or wait until the evening if it was hot.

When he had the restaurant, it was always closed on Sundays. He went to the Roman Catholic Church for earlier mass, then drove home to pick up Dot to take her to the Lutheran Church. Dot had never learned to drive, fearful of the idea. Joe would take her to other church functions, now that he was retired. The church members got so used to seeing Joe that they asked him to become a member. So he did, and was now a member of two churches.

"A Christian is a Christian," Joe would tell his grandchildren. "It doesn't matter which Christian church you are in when praying." Joe looked forward to visits from the grandchildren. His children all lived in different states, the closest was an eight hour drive. Sometimes when the grandkids would come to visit, he would take them to the garden to pick anything that was ready to pick, or have them help him plant seeds. He had a riding mower with a cart attached to the back. He would put the grandkids in the cart and drive them around the yard. Old Joe would have as much fun as the kids. The grandkids knew they would be kept busy when they were at grandpa's. Joe would talk to them as they walked through the garden, picking vegetables, or pulling weeds, or stacking firewood.

"Be a doer, not a sitter," Joe would tell his grandchildren. "Be part of the life around you, don't let it pass you by, just sitting around. I have faith in you children not becoming sitters. Keep being doers."

Whenever he saw his grandchildren he liked to give advice to them, like pointing out the differences between needs and wants. "That figurine on the shelf is a want. The vegetables in the garden are a need. Don't spend all your money on wants, or you will have none left for your needs.... God gave you brains to take care of yourselves and others... You have God-given brains to plan to do the right thing.... Joe would have his words of wisdom for them every visit.

One story he liked to tell them was the story of a boy who almost drowned in the pond behind the house he grew up in. "The boy turned a near tragedy into a positive, by taking swimming lessons. He could have become fearful of water and never gone near it again. But instead, he became a good swimmer, and one day saved someone from drowning."

He would join them on sightseeing trips to historic places, although after his bypass he would only go to places that didn't require too much walking. He liked to take them to Warm Springs where Franklin Roosevelt's cottage was, and where the President died. Roosevelt was Joe's favorite President. Joe told them about places he had been, like Hawaii, New York City, and the Statue of Liberty. "It is a tradition that Wascuras visit the Statue of Liberty. His grandson Philip promised he would go to the Statue.

"It would be neat to fly close over it," Philip said.

"I don't think you can fly close to it," Joe told him. "Not unless you were in an official helicopter or something like that."

Between visits he would call grandchildren to ask about school, and expected to be called whenever they came home with a report card, praising them when they did good, encouraging them when they needed improvement. They looked forward to these calls.

One day in the spring of '94, Joe was working in his garden. Neighbors were cutting down a tree. They asked Joe if he wanted some firewood for his fireplace. "Sure," Joe replied. "Just drop it on my side of the fence."

As Joe turned around with some wood to put on his woodpile, he collapsed. The neighbor, a paramedic, saw him collapse. He and his brother jumped the fence to aid Joe and realized that he needed CPR. They yelled to another relative to call 911, while they performed CPR.

When the ambulance arrived, Dot came out to see what the sirens were about, and saw people bent over Joe, readying him for a trip to the hospital. They were never able to revive Joe.

The funeral was held at the Lutheran Church. In town Joe was still well remembered, a personality in downtown for many years. The line of cars from the Church to the cemetery was many cars long. People from both churches were at the service, including the Catholic priest.

The next week one of Joe's sons wrote a letter to all of the eight grandchildren --

To the grandchildren of Joseph Wascura:

Some of grandpa's grandchildren were still very young when he passed away this year. Someday when you have grandchildren of your own they will ask you about your parents and grandparents, what they did, where they lived, how they lived, and what they were like.

So I am writing this so you can answer those questions about your one Grandpa, the one who would yell "ho, ho, ho," on the phone on Christmas, the one who would swing you on his leg when you were little, the one who always had a hug for you, the one who used the phrase, "you bald headed Elmer," the one with the big Eastern European nose.

Grandpa Joe was born on St Joseph's Day in 1923, thus his name. His father, Walter (Voytek) Wascura, was a Rusyn immigrant who immigrated to the United States in 1899 from Ostruna, Austro-Hungary (Slovakia today). His mother, Dorotha Djurkan was a Slovak immigrant also from Austro-Hungary. Walter was a coal miner in Swoyersville, Pennsylvania, where they lived on Kossack St where many Eastern European immigrants lived. Joe was the youngest of six children. Walter had brothers and sisters that also immigrated and settled in Chicago and New Jersey.

Growing up in the 1930s, was not always easy because of the economic depression, and the miners would not always have work. As a result many boys and girls would have to quit school at 15 or 16 and go to work, as Grandpa had to do at 16.

After World War II broke out, Grandpa went into the Navy and became a coxswain on the USS New Jersey battleship. He served in the Lookout Company and the ship was part of the fleet that bombed enemy islands along the Pacific.

When the war ended Joe married Grandma Dot. She was one of seven children. While his was an immigrant Catholic family, she was of old German American families who could trace their roots back to some of the original German Lutheran settlers in Pennsylvania. Like many other World War II veterans Joe and grandma joined the baby boom, having two boys and two girls, your parents.

Grandpa supported his family by working in the restaurant industry in northeastern Pennsylvania, Chicago and Georgia. It was Grandpa's and Grandma's dream for their children to go to college. So in 1964 they moved to the Midwest to improve their income.

Grandpa and grandma were always proud of the fact that all four of their children graduated from college. Eventually they moved south and grandpa bought his own restaurant. Some of you grandchildren remember going there to eat lunch when you were there on vacation. Many of the people in town got to know Joe from eating at his restaurant. Eventually Grandpa sold his restaurant and retired.

Around his 71st birthday you could find Grandpa out back, as usual, helping grandchildren chop wood, often swinging the ax in instruction and example. Much had changed in his live since his younger days, when the average man never thought that in a few years, television, computers, and a man on the moon would be part of our lives.

He would still bellow out a deep hello to customers, fellow church goers, friends, and always with a smile. Many people came to his funeral. People knew him for his friendly hello and smile.

He has left a rich legacy to his grandchildren. It is the example he set by the way he lived his life. He didn't feel it was necessary to swear and didn't. He was privately religious, honest, quick to smile, and quick to offer a friendly hello. People respected Joe. The most important thing to him was his family.

All his family will miss his "ho, ho, ho," this Christmas. But we are blessed because he is in our hearts and our minds. We are rich with his memory. He is part of us and we are better for it.

Chapter Fourteen

College

When Ivan's son, Simon, graduated from college at the University of Presov with a degree in pre-med in 2002, he applied to the Slovak Medical University in Bratislava. He was confident he would be accepted, having scored high on the entrance exams. But as with most students, he wondered how he could ever pay for med school. When he went to Bratislava to take the tests, there was a display at the entrance to the testing room, with brochures from the army medical corps. The Slovak Army was in need of doctors and would pay for medical school if you served in the army for a minimum of six years after med school and internship.

After he passed the tests and was accepted, he signed up for the army program. With the pressure of med school studies, he didn't need the added worry of large student loans.

At the campus in Bratislava, there were many female nursing students. Simon had plenty of opportunities for dates and would offer to help young ladies study. Simon was afraid to get serious with just one girl. With many years of studying to do, plus a future internship and residency, he was afraid to commit. He only had so much time. If he felt a relationship getting too serious, he would back off and date someone else.

Standing almost six feet tall, slender, with big shoulders, and dark wavy hair, the girls found him attractive. He felt that with so many young ladies around, why settle for just one.

There was, however, one girl he wished he had never let get away. Her name was Helen. She was a short brunette with soft brown eyes, medium length hair, and a charming smile. She lived in a town near Osturna, but they had gone to the same high school. She was a bright student who, like Simon, was interested in a medical career. They sat next to each other in both biology and math class. They dated, and though she wasn't the first girl he kissed, she was the first that he felt was the only girl for him; the one he enjoyed being with more than anyone.

At the end of high school, Helen received a scholarship to the nursing school in Bratislava and Simon received a scholarship to the University of Presov in pre-med. After their graduation, Simon gave Helen his football (soccer) pin. He had received the pin for being the captain of the school's football team.

"Wear this pin to show that you are my girl," Simon suggested, smiling with hope.

"You mean, if I wear this, we will not date anyone else?" Helen asked.

"Right, just each other when we come home between semesters."

"I have to think about that Simon."

"What's there to think about?" he asked, his smile now gone.

"Will you be dating no one else?" she asked, ignoring his question.

"Of course not."

"I think we should be able to see other people," Helen suggested. "We will still be able to see each other between semesters when we are home. We both have years of education to do, especially you."

Simon was disappointed. He had figured that she would be his constant companion, despite the miles between them; spending their time together between semesters. Helen was driven to get her bachelor degree in nursing. She would be the first in her family to graduate from college.

"Helen, you know how I feel, and I hope you will someday reconsider. The pin is yours to keep," Simon said. Their colleges were far apart, being at opposite ends of Slovakia.

Over the next four years, they did see each other between semesters when they were both home. During school they would talk by phone at least twice a week. After they each graduated with bachelor degrees, Helen got a job at a hospital near Bratislava.

When Simon passed his medical school entrance exams, he called Helen with the news. "Maybe we can share an apartment between where you will be working and the medical school," Simon suggested.

"We both need to be close to work and school," Helen declined. "You will need time to study. You won't have time to commute. Besides,I already got an apartment next to the hospital, and have a roommate."

Simon had hoped to soon become engaged to Helen. "Who is your roommate? Have I met her?"

"It is not a she. It's my fiancé," Helen said slowly, almost in a whisper.

"Fiancé? When did this happen?"

"We've been dating for months."

"When did you plan to tell me?"

"When you got to Bratislava."

Simon didn't know what to say. He just sat on the chair on his parent's porch in Osturna thinking of what to say next. Finally he said, "You didn't say anything when I saw you last week when I went to Bratislava to take the exams."

"I had little time to see you that day, as I had to get to work," Helen answered in a whimpering whisper, almost crying. "I didn't want to take your mind off of the test. I had only said yes to him the day before, and we were busy looking for an apartment."

"My mom is calling me to dinner," Simon lied. "See you sometime in Bratislava." He hung up before he might cry. He didn't want her to know that he felt like crying. She was an attractive, intelligent woman who many men would be happy to have as a wife, and it didn't look like it would be him.

During his entire first year of medical school, though busy with studies, he dated as many women as he had time for, hoping he might run into Helen with a beautiful date next to him. He compared everyone he dated to Helen, and they couldn't measure up in his eyes. He never talked to her again and she never called.

#######

One day, after his avionics class at the engineering building, Joe's grandson, Philip, headed to the student union for lunch when he saw an army Kiowa helicopter land on the grass in the center of campus. Intrigued, Philip walked around the helicopter after the rotors had stopped, asking the pilots technical questions about it. After majoring in Aviation Technology at Embry-Riddle Aeronautical University for almost four years, he was wishing to have an opportunity to fly after graduation.

Most students at the university were engineering or technology majors. Less than 25% were flight students majoring in aeronautical science and minoring in flight. 25% were international students. Philip had studied airframe, powerplant, and avionics and now as a senior, would be graduating in May with a Bachelor of Science degree in Aviation Technology.

The highly rated Embry-Riddle University was the Harvard or Yale of aviation. All majors were related to aviation. Parts of the campus were unique for a college campus. One large classroom had many propellers in it. Another had aircraft instruments and avionics. One classroom had pieces of wings, while another classroom had several turbine engines in various stages of disassembly. One class that Philip had taken, required students in teams of three to disassemble a turbine engine, put it back together, then take it to a firing building where they had to hook it up to controls and run the engine from a control room. The building had an air intake at one end and an exhaust chute that funneled exhaust out the roof.

Unfortunately for the male Embry-Riddle students, only 20% of the students were women. However, the female students were happy with the ratio. A good-looking female student would have the attention of men all the time. In many of Philip's classes there would often be only one girl, and some classes had no female students at all. One attractive blond woman in one of his electrical engineering classes would have the door opened for her all the time. Men would hurry to the classroom door to see who would hold it open for her. This female student never had to open a classroom door – ever; they would be waiting for her. At Embry-Riddle they had a saying; men get "Embry-Riddle eyes", which meant all female students look good.

Philip's roommate was an aeronautical science major with an Air Force ROTC minor. He would be graduating as a second lieutenant and would be going to air force flight school after graduation and hoped to be flying F16 fighter jets. He had told Philip that all the military flight school slots would be taken by ROTC and academy graduates.

Since Philip was not an ROTC student, if he went into the Air Force, he would not be going to flight school after officer candidate school. His roommate said it was the same for the Navy and Marines. But Philip might have a chance at Army or Coast Guard helicopter flight school. So when Philip saw the Kiowa helicopter he saw his chance to talk to the Army about being a pilot.

After he was shown around the helicopter by the pilots, Philip talked to the recruiter and asked for a brochure. "Most pilots in the Army are warrant officers," the recruiter told him. "The Army has a need for infantry and armored officers. So after commissioned officer school few are sent to flight school. You won't have a choice. They will assign you to advanced training as they have needs. Are you wanting to go in the army to be a pilot?"

"Yes," Philip replied. "If I can't be a pilot then I don't want to go in."

"Then you need to go in as a warrant officer," the recruiter suggested. "You would go to warrant officer candidate school, then you would go directly to flight school after graduating. In fact the WOCS and flight school are both at Ft Rucker in Alabama. Warrant officers are specialists. Your primary duty will be to fly. The pay is similar to commissioned officer pay, except that pilots get flight pay in addition."

"Sounds interesting," Philip said.

"You will need to be given a physical. Shouldn't be a problem. You look athletic. If you pass that we can set you up to get started after you graduate."

After learning about aircraft for four years, Philip was anxious to fly aircraft instead just analyzing it, so he signed up to go into the army after graduation to become a pilot.

The aviation industry is male dominated, as is military aviation. So, despite being handsome with light brown hair, blue eyes, and an athletic physic, Philip attended a college with few women, and now was headed to military aviation where he would have even fewer opportunities to meet women.

Just before graduation, the Iraq war started in March 2003. Few expected it to last long.

The graduation was held on the lawn of campus so there could be a flyover during the ceremony of military jets from nearby Patrick Air Force base and some old restored aircraft flown by alumni. After the ceremony it was tradition for graduates to have their picture taken in front of the full size statue of the original Wright flyer with one Wright brother on the plane and one standing next to it.

Chapter Fifteen

Afghanistan 2010

NATO doctor Simon Smolenak arrived on a transport plane to Camp Marmal, located next to the Mazir-i-Sharif airport in Afghanistan. The tarmac was blistering hot on this early September day, heat radiating up as the sun radiated down to cook his body. He moved quickly to get to the headquarters building to check in with his CO.

Slovakia had been a member of NATO since 2004 and as a member, they needed to supply a certain number of troops each year. His surgical residency had taken place in both England and Slovakia, then the Slovak Army assigned him to NATO for two years, which sent him to Afghanistan.

His company's office was located in a steel building next to the larger steel hospital building. The temperature was about 80 inside, which was about all an AC system could lower it to, being it was over 100 outside. With this camp located in the mountains, he could only imagine how much hotter is was in the lower altitudes in Afghanistan. After finishing his paperwork, he was shown to his room, which was to be shared with a fellow Slovak, a medic Sargent, who was on duty at the moment. All medical personnel were housed in a wing of the hospital.

After putting away his belongings in a locker, he went to one of the cafeterias in a nearby steel building, called the atrium, for dinner. He had a choice of an American cafeteria or a German one. He wanted to meet non-Europeans, so he chose the American cafeteria. All personnel were required to wash their hands at the entrance to the cafeteria.

After going through the chow line he looked for a place to sit. He saw a US officer sitting at an empty table, his head bowed, hands clasped, and obviously saying grace quietly to himself. Simon sat across from the officer and bowed his head and clasped his hands quietly to say grace, as was his custom. When he looked up after blessing himself, the officer was looking at him.

"Hello," the American officer said smiling. "I don't recognize the uniform Captain. It's not German or Norwegian."

"Slovakia," Simon answered. His Slovakia Velcro label was half falling off making it unreadable.

"I see the medical insignia," the officer observed. "Are you a doctor?"

"Yes," Simon answered, fixing the Velcro label on his camouflage fatigues. "I've been assigned to NATO and they sent me here. I see by your wings that you are a pilot. The United States handles the medivac here, doesn't it?"

"Yes. We handle all medivac and armed support of the medivac. I pilot a UH60 helicopter. I'm Philip Wascura." He extended his hand to shake.

Simon shook his hand. "Simon Smolenak. Is that a lieutenant bar?"

"Chief Warrant Officer. Most US helicopter pilots are Warrant Officers. Specialist officers. How long have you been here?"

"Two hours."

"You speak English well."

"I did some of my medical training in England."

Three other men came to the table.

"Captain, this is my copilot Captain Griesemer, my crew chief Art and my medic Ben," Philip introduced his crew. "Men this is Captain Smolenak, a Slovak doctor just assigned to NATO." Simon noticed Art's name badge said Harper and Ben's said Klaczko.

"Call me Val," Captain Griesemer said to Simon. "Are the Germans and Norwegians running out of doctors?"

"Maybe so," Simon guessed. "But I am a surgeon. There is always a demand for good army surgeons."

"Things have been quiet around here lately," Philip said. "But you can count on our company to get the injured here quickly. Our company has the quickest response time."

After eating, Simon went to the hospital to meet some of the staff, and met his roommate, Danjo Djurkan. The camp was made up of several long steel buildings and numerous tents surrounded with plenty of trucks, Humvees, helicopters, and other aircraft. The steel buildings housed the hospital, command center, flight command, the atrium with cafeterias and rec center, aircraft maintenance hangers, and other special purpose buildings. The air conditioned tents were sleeping quarters for troops designed to house ten men but most averaged 18.

The camp was located in the far north central of Afghanistan near the city of Mazir-i-sharif. It sat on a flat plateau at 1260 ft elevation. A few miles to the north were high mountains.

The NATO forces were made up of personnel from seventeen nations, with the US and Germany having the most troops. The camp provided security for nine provisional areas and supplied five reconstruction teams. It acted as a medical center for forces and locals. A bazaar was located inside the camp for locals to sell items like afghan rugs, electronics, and small wooden items.

A few years earlier, when the Americans were sending medivac units there after the German Army had opened the camp, they realized that the Germans had a beer bar. The Americans had a policy of no alcohol in a combat zone and no alcohol in a Muslim country. The Germans said they go nowhere without their beer, and couldn't live without it. So the US Army decided to compromise. The Germans could have their beer bar, but it could only be open certain hours. Anyone in the bar must be off duty and could not be in there four hours before going on duty. No Americans were allowed in the bar or receiving any beer from the bar.

The next morning was Sunday, and Simon went to a US Army chapel service. He knew English better then German or Norwegian. He saw Philip so he sat next to him. After the service he and Philip invited the Chaplin to lunch.

As they ate, the Chaplin asked them each what denomination church they attended when at home. Philip told them about a non-denominational Christian church he liked in Texas. He liked the young adult bible study group that met weekly.

"Was it a good place to meet single young ladies," the Chaplin asked smiling.

"Yes," Philip agreed. "Sometimes."

"That is how I met my wife," the Chaplin said.

Simon said he enjoyed the church at his small village where he grew up. "I guess it is because I know everyone who goes to the church, which is the entire village, because it is the only church in town. It is a Ruthenian Greek Catholic Church. The priest and his wife and children are good friends with my family."

"I thought priests don't marry?" Philip asked.

"You are thinking of Roman Catholic priests," Simon said. "The eastern Greek Orthodox churches are different. Services were never in Latin, and if an orthodox priest wants to marry, he has to do so before being ordained. He is not allowed to after.

How big is your village?" the Chaplin asked.

"Around four hundred people," Simon estimated. "It is next to the Tatra Mountains National Park. The village used to have more residents, so there are empty old homes that are rented out to tourists who are hiking or skiing the mountains. A good place to visit."

After lunch Simon asked Philip to show him one of the medivac helicopters. "I want to see how yours is set up," Simon told him.

Philip showed him the medical equipment set up in the back. The UH60Q Blackhawk helicopter had a six patient litter system with onboard oxygen, airway management capability, patient monitoring equipment, and storage of intravenous solutions. Impressed, Simon then asked if he could sit in the pilot's seat.

"Sure," Philip said. "You can't do any harm as long as it's on the ground."

"So many instruments," Simon observed as he sat in the seat.

"We have an all-weather radar system and a forward looking infrared turret to allow rescue missions to be carried out in all weather and terrains," Philip explained.

Philip started describing what each instrument was, but the terminology was unfamiliar to Simon as he was sure some medical terms and equipment were unfamiliar to Philip.

"I am impressed with the roomy space and the equipment in the back for your crew," Simon said.

"The UH60 medivac version is one of the best built medical choppers in the world," Philip explained. "We fly at 150 to 160 knots, but it can go faster."

"Where are the guns?"

"No guns. In the back we have shorty M-16s in case we crash, we can grab them for protection. We usually have an armed helicopter escorting us, like an Apache. In an emergency we always have an escort. If it is just a transport, like we are taking a patient from one hospital to another, then we may not."

"Do you think I could go along on a flight sometime?"

"I don't see why not. You'll have to find someone's helmet that fits you and a flight suit that fits. We can find someone your size that you can borrow from. The flight uniforms we wear are made of a different material that is fire resistant. You just have to Velcro your name and Slovak Army or NATO label on."

Philip was a command pilot. He had been in the Army over seven years now. Most Army pilots are Warrant Officers, who are specialists, with flying as their primary assignment, so they fly more often than commissioned officers. By 2009, Philip had enough flight hours to be a command pilot. His skills as a pilot and his degree in Aviation Technology got him sent to test pilot school, and he was now his company's maintenance test pilot. A year and a half earlier he had been in Iraq for a year. He preferred flying medivac where they were part of the process of saving lives, instead of in an attack helicopter, or moving supplies, or troops.

It took more skills to fly medivac. When flying in a war zone you would have to find a spot to land, sometimes between buildings, and sometimes trying not to land on bodies, trusting the person on the ground to direct you. More skill is needed as a helicopter pilot than a fixed wing pilot. A helicopter pilot has to control foot pedals, while one hand controls the stick and the other controls throttle. It takes coordination of mind, body, and machine.

Flying medivac brought the crews to situations where a firefight or explosion had just taken place. The pilots would ask the ground if the LZ was hot or cold, as they approached the scene. Hot meant that the area was still under fire. Cold meant that there was no firefight at that moment. If it was cold they would start looking for a place to land, which could be a challenge. Sometimes they would have to land wherever there was room, and the wounded had to be driven or carried to where they had landed. One of the first medivac calls Philip was on in Iraq was a bad scene on a busy street. There was enough room to land, and as the medics readied the wounded to transport, the pilots looked out at a scene of body parts and dead Army soldiers and civilians. Trucks were being sent to pick up the dead, as the medics loaded the wounded on the chopper and apache attack helicopters circled above.

The medivac crews rotated 24 hours on duty, 24 hours on call, and 24 hours off duty. Sometimes on his off days, Philip would have to do a maintenance test flight to see if the repairs solved a helicopter's problem.

During the summer, the tarmac would be 140 degrees. The crews would be relieved when they lifted off to escape the heat radiating off the tarmac to fly through the cooler air above. In the winter the temperatures were close to freezing at Camp Marmal because of their altitude.

Simon would look for Philip or his crew when he went to meals. One time, at lunch with some of Philip's crew, Simon was commenting on American last names. "So many American last names are European," he observed.

"Well, unless you are Native American, our ancestors came from somewhere else," Philip said.

"We have a German doctor named Griesemer here at the hospital, the same last name as Val," Simon said.

"My ancestors came over in the early 1700s from Germany," Val pointed out.

"You two might be distant cousins," Simon concluded.

"Very, very distant," Val laughed.

"Your last name sounds eastern European, Philip," Simon observed.

"Well, my great grandparents came over from villages in the eastern European mountains," Philip agreed.

"The Carpathian Mountains?" Simon asked.

"I am not sure," Philip said.

"You could have cousins there," Simon realized.

"Distant," Philip said.

"My grandfather came over to America from Poland after World War II," Ben joined in the conversation. "South Poland, not far from the Carpathian Mountains. During the war he had to hide from the Germans because he was Jewish and a Rusyn Orthodox Catholic family helped him hide. He had to pretend to be a Rusyn cousin of the family and go to the Christian Church with the villagers to appear non-Jewish."

"My grandparents told me a story of hiding people during the war," Simon related.

"Maybe they crossed paths," Ben said.

"Maybe," Simon agreed. "We being here may prevent another larger war. I treat Afghans every day and they just want peace. They know the economy is much better when there is no repression. Coming from a country that had been repressed by commies for 40 years, the economy did get better when we got rid of the commies."

"We ought to go visit you in Slovakia whenever you get back to your mountains," Ben suggested.

"I don't live in the village because I live wherever the Army has me stationed," Simon explained. "But I do own a very old small house in my village. The village has only about one fourth the number of people it had 100 years ago, but the houses are still there. My dad owns a couple old small furnished log houses and rents them out to tourists who come to hike the Tatra Mountains or ski in the winter. So there is always a place to stay whether I am there or not."

"Sounds like a plan," Philip said. "Make sure we exchange addresses and emails before we leave, Simon."

"I would like to visit America someday," Simon told them. "So many people from my village moved to America in the past hundred years. I'd like to see the Rocky Mountains,

Florida beaches, the Smithsonian Museums, and the Statue of Liberty."

"Let us know when and we can be your hosts," Philip offered. "You know, I once flew a Blackhawk over the Statue of Liberty."

"That must have been awesome," Art said.

"It was when I was stationed outside of D.C., and I had to fly to a helipad near the New York docks," Philip explained. "We flew right over the Statue. We had to pick up a general and a high ranking defense department official and fly them to D.C."

"That sounds like better duty then flying around Afghanistan," Val pointed out.

On Christmas Day, Simon did not see Philip at the Chapel service, so he walked over to flight command. Philip and his crew were on duty and lying around hoping they wouldn't get a call. One was taking a nap, two others were watching a DVD movie and Philip was checking the weather report. "Are you off duty today," Philip asked Simon when he saw him come in.

"Yes," Simon said. "By the way I've found a helmet that fits and a flight uniform I can borrow."

"Normally we have a medic trainee for Ben to work with, but today we have just Ben so there is room for you if you want," Philip offered.

"Great," Simon enthusiastically. "I'll go get them. I'll be right back."

"No promises," Philip said. "Probably won't be getting any calls."

While Simon was gone, the communications officer got a call. "Four Afghan policemen have gotten ambushed north of here, northeast of Kholm on a mountain side," he told Philip. "Problem is, it was a cell phone call, not a radio call."

"Sounds like a trap," Philip suspected.

"I've got Apache pilots being alerted now," the officer said. "I requested two to fly ahead and circle the area."

"How many injured," Philip asked.

"Three of the four," the officer said. "One bad enough that they don't want to move him."

"See if you can get a more exact location," Val requested, quickly working on the flight plan, as Philip ran out the door to start up the engines.

As the crew went to the helicopter, they met Simon coming in. "We have a call," Philip told him. "But it may be dangerous, so you can back out if you want."

"I assumed they were all dangerous," Simon said. "I'll go."

288

Simon sat next to Ben as Philip and Val got in their pilot seats. Art was outside pulling the blocks from the wheels. "Are they doing the preflight check?" Simon asked Ben.

"No. Preflight check is done when we come on duty," Ben explained. "That way, when we get a call, we just go after bringing the engines up to speed. We will have to wait, though, for the Apache pilots to get airborne and give them a head start. They will circle the landing zone before advising us to land."

Simon could see two apaches taking off from another area of the camp. A couple of minutes later Philip increased the throttle and they took off. Simon was surprised at how quick the Blackhawk climbed in altitude. Its two turboshaft engines loudly took the 64 foot helicopter on a steep climb. Simon could hear Philip talking to the control tower on his helmet. It was a chilly day in the 40s on the ground, and would be colder at the higher mountain where they were headed.

"How long will it take to get there?" Simon asked Ben in a yell over the noise of the engines.

"It's far, probably over twenty minutes at full speed," Ben estimated.

When they approached the area they could see the Apaches circling between two mountain peaks. The mountains in north Afghanistan had little vegetation, but despite that there were plenty of rocks to hide behind. Philip circled, waiting for the Apaches advice to land.

The Apaches radioed that they could see no insurgents, but plenty of places for them to hide. They said that there was a spot on the road wide enough for the Blackhawk to land near the police SUV. They could see two police lying on the ground with two others looking over them.

Philip lowered the Blackhawk down on the narrow road, the rotors close to the mountainside. Dirt and sand blew up all around them, as Art leaned out the door, calling out the feet left to touch down.

"Let's make this quick," Philip said. "No telling how many are aiming rifles at us." As he said that one of the four men came running at them with a weapon, motioning them to follow him.

Simon and Ben jumped out with medical bags. Art grabbed a litter, as Val jumped out and grabbed another. Philip kept his hands and feet on the controls so as to be ready to take off, if necessary, circle, and land again if he is shot at. Usually the two pilots stayed in the chopper and took off, circling until the medic as ready for them to land. Nothing was routine about this call.

Simon realized that the one policeman was already dead, so he got to work on the other one lying on the road who had a head wound. He did an initial dressing of the wound, got him on the stretcher and told Art and Val to get him on the chopper. He then helped Ben with the third policeman who had leg and arm wounds. They got him loaded on the chopper as the fourth policeman helped Art get the dead policeman on a stretcher and on the chopper. Val jumped back into his pilot seat and they took off.

"We've got to get this one patient to a hospital quick," Simon told everyone. "Very, very quick." Simon continued to tend to the policeman as they flew.

Val radioed base for a location of an Afghan hospital possibly closer than the camp hospital. "Time is important," he told them. Command radioed back the GPS location of an Afghan hospital close to them in Kholm. Val told command to call the hospital and tell them to be ready in a few minutes.

When they reached the hospital, Philip and Val flew around the hospital looking for a place to land. The hospital was on the side of a mountain. They saw a man in a white coat waving his arms. The space where the man stood was tight, with the walls of the hospital on one side and the wall of another building on the opposite side. The third side was the side of the mountain and a dirt road on the fourth side to form a small landing zone, which had probably never been used for the purpose of a helicopter landing.

Val opened the door next to him and leaned out, as Art opened the door on the other side and leaned out while attached to a strap. As Philip lowered the chopper, dirt and sand blew up so much, he couldn't see anything. The man in the white coat disappeared. Val and Art told Philip they could not see the ground. Children that had been playing on the dirt road ran to get away from the blowing dirt and sand.

When Philip felt a wheel touch the ground, he let it down. He had to disengage the clutch to let the rotors slow down, because of all the sand blowing up. Simon and Ben grabbed the policeman with the head wound first. Inside, the doctor waved them into the operating room where they slid him on the operating table. Simon explained what they must do, hoping they understood him talking English with a Slovak accent. The other wounded policeman was brought in as well as the dead one.

The Apaches were still circling overhead as Philip engaged the rotors after his crew got back in. "This bird needs to go through the car wash," Val said as they headed back. Everything in and out of the Blackhawk was covered with over an inch of sand.

"Thank God we had Dr Smolenak with us," Ben said. "He may have saved that policeman's life."

When they radioed base that they were on the way back, base said they had some visitors to welcome them back. "Is it OK to bring them out to the chopper when you get here?"

"Negative," Philip said. "We are dirty." Dirty meant that the chopper needed to be pressure washed with disinfectant because of blood. Of course with all the sand and dirt inside one couldn't tell for sure if any blood was beneath the sand, but Philip figured better safe than sorry.

When Philip landed the chopper next to the maintenance hangar so it could be pressure washed, he noticed several people in jog suits watching and talking to the smiling communications officer. When Philip and the crew walked to flight command, they noticed the jog suits said New England Patriots on them and they were all young ladies.

"Now this is what I call a welcome," Val said grinning.

The attractive girls shook hands with each of the smiling crew and invited them to come watch them cheer later that evening at a show at the cafeteria. The New England Patriots had over 30 cheerleaders and each December they would send 6 of them with the USO to entertain troops for ten days, touring around to some bases.

"We should be getting off duty about then," Val said as he accepted the invitation. "I will be in a front seat ladies."

"We need cheerleaders like this for our football teams," Simon said later that evening at the show.

"You mean your soccer teams, don't you?" Philip asked.

"Oh, yes, I forgot," Simon said. "You call football, soccer, and you call the pointy ball you throw with your arm, a football. So confusing."

Simon and Val talked to the cheerleaders after the show, learning their names and promising to visit them whenever they visited the Boston area, when their deployments were finished. The girls told them they could get

293

in touch with them through the Patriots office, when in the area. Even though Val lived in Texas where he was stationed, his family lived in Pennsylvania, so he planned to visit Boston the next time he was visiting family.

Over the next few months, Simon taught the crew some Slovak and Rusyn words and the Americans helped him get better with English. They would meet to play ping pong or pool at the rec enter. Philp's dad recorded TV shows and sent the DVDs to him. Everyone would watch them on their laptop computers at a table at the rec center or in their tent.

Occasionally they would play tag football or soccer on a grassless field. On Super Bowl Sunday, February 2011, they all got up real early to watch the game live on armed forces TV. After watching Green Bay beat Pittsburgh, many soldiers went out to toss the football around. Philip showed Simon how to throw the football. To everyone's surprise Simon had a good strong arm, but he couldn't catch the 'pointy ball' as he called it. They started a touch football game with Ben as quarterback and Philip as receiver. Simon was told to rush the other team's quarterback.

Some Germans were watching and challenged the soldiers to a soccer game; Germans versus all other countries. The Germans figured they had an easy game, but were surprised when Simon and his roommate Danjo combined for several goals. The score was tied at four goals each when they realized some of them had to go on duty, and that ended the game.

One day, several soldiers were sitting around the rec center eating ice cream and talking about women. They talked about wives, ex-wives, girlfriends, and ex-girlfriends. Art was married with children. Ben was engaged. Philip, Val and Simon were each single and between girlfriends. During previous wars soldiers wrote to loved ones. The Iraq and Afghanistan Wars were cell phone wars. Soldiers were given donated cell phones to call home. No longer needing to wait weeks for letters to go back and forth, it was instant communication verbally. You just had to remember the time difference so you didn't call someone when they were asleep.

"You remember me telling you about my girlfriend in college?" Simon asked Philip as he ate the last of his ice cream. "Her name was Helen."

"Yeah," Philip replied.

"I got a letter from my sister saying she saw her," Simon told his friends. "Turns out, she divorced that bum she married after only a year, and has been single since. My sister said she was asking all about me."

"You should write her," Philip said. "Nothing ventured nothing gained."

"I could ask about how her family is doing," Simon figured. "I think I'll call her when I get back."

"Why not ask your sister to get her phone number from her family," Philip suggested. "Then call her up and say – 'this is Dr. Smolenak calling from Afghanistan; I have a spare minute to give you any medical advice; do you have any questions?'"

Simon laughed. "That would be a shock for her to get a call from Afghanistan."

At the end of May it was time for Philip's crew to leave. On Philip's last Sunday in camp, he talked to Simon after the church service during lunch. "I won't miss this food," Philip commented. "When I get home I'm going to go to the grocery store and get some chocolate milk, steak, and some pyrohies."

"Pyrohies?" Simon asked.

"Yeah," Philip replied.

"That is one of the favorite food of Slovaks and Rusyn, and you pronounce it like a Slovak or Rusyn, pyrohy. Not pierogi which is Polish. You definitely have Eastern European heritage."

"My mom learned to cook them from my dad's mom, who learned to make them from my grandfather's mom who was born in the old country. When you come to the United States, we have all kinds of ethnic restaurants, food styles from all over the world."

We definitely must go to each other's countries," Simon said. "We have become good friends. It is like we are cousins, like we are related, even though you can't speak your great grandparent's language." They laughed and promised each other to keep in touch.

As they walked out of the cafeteria, the winds blew mildly, coming from the mountains with a pleasing smell of rare mountain trees and flowers, refreshing the air like a promise of better life ahead.

Epilogue

With the changing borders and changing governments of the past 120 years the Rusyn, have integrated into the societies of other countries in North America and Europe. Through intermarrying with other nationalities today most Rusyn are just part Rusyn, so they identify with the nation they live in, whether it be Slovakia, Ukraine, Poland, or the US.

Today 750,000 Americans can trace their ancestry to Rusyns. There are over 1.5 million Rusyns in Europe today, about 120,000 in Slovakia. Three quarters of European Rusyns live in the Carpathian Mountains of Ukraine. Over 200,000 Rusyn immigrated to the US from 1880 to 1914, settling in Pennsylvania, New Jersey, Chicago, and Ohio. People brought their Christian denominations with them. Ruthenian Catholic churches are found throughout the US. Some still hold church services in Slavonic.

In Slovakia today Christians are Roman Catholic, Lutheran, Eastern Orthodox, and Greek Catholic. Today Slovakia uses the Roman alphabet, not Cyrillic. People in Osturna speak Slovak and Rusyn is spoken less. The towns of Osturna and Klenov each have less than 400 people today.

The Rusyn were hardy farmers of the hills. During the early 1900s small farming communities in Europe and America got smaller as industrialization of agriculture required less manpower to produce crops, resulting in larger farms and less labor. Rural families moved to cities where there were better opportunities, resulting in the migration from Europe to America between the 1880s and 1914. Generations later, families have descendants in both the US and Europe, but do not know of the whereabouts of each other.

In the modern world, one can never tell when someone you meet may have a common ancestor with you. In most cases, the two of you would never realize it. But we do have one thing in common; we all have optimism in us, to look forward to better days ahead.

Authors Note

The Carpatho-Rusyn Society website, c-rs,org, has a good map of the areas of eastern Europe highlighted as to where Rusyn people had lived. The western most highlighted area in Slovakia is where Osturna is. The National Carpatho-Rusyn Culture Center is located at 915 Dickson St. Munhall, PA.

The National Slovak Society, nsslife,org, has a museum at 351 Valley Brook Rd. McMurray, PA.

The website, the Carpathian Connection, tccweb.org., has a video of the village of Osturna today, information about the village, pictures of St Michael Church, and roadside chapels. At the website, go to Our People, then click on Carpatho-Rusyn Villages, then click on Osturna.

About the Author

Fred Wascura grew up in northeast Pennsylvania and Chicago and graduated from the University of Wisconsin-Whitewater. He has lived since in Florida for over forty years.

Blog – cyclingloopsandlighthouses.blogspot.com